STARBORNE

a novel

ALEPH KATZ

Relax. Read. Repeat.

STARBORNE
By Aleph Katz
Published by TouchPoint Press
Brookland, AR 72417
www.touchpointpress.com

Softcover ISBN: 978-1-956851-65-6

Editor: Scott Bury
Cover Design: ColbieMyles.com
Cover image: Smart city with skyscrapers and interconnectivity by Vina (Adobe Stock)

Visit the author's website at www.alephkatz.com

First Edition

Printed in the United States of America.

To all who are still searching for where they belong.

CHAPTER 1

I've never had trouble jumping fences. It's a simple climb and a jump. Take a leap of faith, and before you know it, you've reached the other side. Sure, sometimes there will be a thornbush or an angry dog on the other side, but that's never stopped me. You have to have trust in yourself. Just . . . jump.

Hopping the fence beside my home, I make my way to the police precinct. I glance around, nose up, shoulders back. I meet other people's glances with nasty glares. *Mysterious and untouchable*, I think with my usual smirk. The lives of the average are nothing like mine. Girls walk on the street, dancing over their own legs, acting like they have somewhere important to be when they don't. Their faces are absolutely *covered* with foundation that they are going to wipe off when the day is done, and their eyelashes are longer than any animal I have seen. Bright, unnatural colors are painted across their lips, like a glimmering sunrise that won't seem to fade. Jesus, it's a circus, and everyone wants to be the main attraction.

The only thing I can stand about those pompous teenage girls is their perfume. The aroma is the same as the roses my mom orders through the mail.

The average thirteen-to-nineteen-year-old girl lives as a faker. Well, every thirteen-to-nineteen-year-old girl but me. I know I have to be different. I know I *am* different. The world wouldn't make sense if I were in the same barrel with the rest of them. Besides, why should I need to hide behind some mask? I'm fine with my naked face. It's real.

"Instant savings!"

"Limited offer!"

"Try this cream, you'll never need a doctor again!"

Billboards flash a different promotion every eight seconds, hungry for attention. But the flashy presentations don't catch my eye. I know where my priorities lie.

The precinct comes into view.

My watch reads 11:17 in the morning. Fashionably late. That's how I like it. It establishes a sense of power, something I need to maintain in this building. The door dings approvingly and slides open with a "kssh" as my familiar figure approaches it. Everything is as it was the day before, and the day before that. Every day for the past year, a living hell.

The world should work in one way—constantly moving forward. But in a police precinct, it's the opposite. It feels like I've gone back in time. An old analog clock ticks above the desk of Ms. Honey Adler. You'd think it was a fabricated name, made for a woman hiding out in witness protection, but it's just. too. real. And the worst part is, she's as sickeningly sweet as her name suggests.

"Good morning, Charlotte!" Her eyes and nose crinkle when she sees me, her bouncy golden hair flinging in every direction. Imagine Goldilocks working a desk job. I open my mouth to respond when an unpleasant, familiar voice snags my attention.

"Charlie Starborne. Late as always, aren't ya?" I throw a casual, sideways glance at Orson. His face is unshaven, and his unwrinkled shirt is tucked in. Every aspect of his appearance is double- and triple-checked. He probably stands in the mirror every morning, gawking at his wide shoulders and crooked smile to ensure his hyena-like personality matches the body it inhabits.

He glares at me with that stupid, gap-toothed smile, and I want to sink into the bleak walls surrounding me. Orson looks like he's planning my death. I would usually dismiss this as the hyena in his brain acting up, but he has a twitch in his eye that says *you better not screw things up today*. I have no idea what the stink-eye is for. I should ignore him, go sit in the back and file papers until the clock tells me I'm home free.

Instead, I turn to him, cross my arms, and fake a smile. The smile contorts into a mocking sneer. I can't help myself. He returns a similar expression.

This relationship can be described in one word: enemies. It is no secret that we can't stand each other. Orson and I stand-off in a western style drawing battle, waiting for the other to make a move, draw a gun.

Ms. Adler watches us. She leans forward, knocking over a pen holder with her arm. My life, to her, is a soap opera. Another excuse to distract her from filing papers. When the sneering becomes too much to bear, she clears her throat. Orson's eyes move to her as mine stay glaring at him. He's not my boss, despite the fine print on every legal document.

"Yes, Ms. Adler?" Orson says, adjusting his tie. "I hope this is worth my time." Honey stares wide-eyed at him. She has no power here. Her soap opera is over. Roll credits.

"Charlie needs to sign in for the day, sir," she replies.

I nearly forgot. The pen touches the paper. *Pens are such useless tools. Ink is for cavemen.* Digital cubes are much easier to use. They can immediately print or send anything in seconds. Easy, efficient, and simple. The way all things should be. "May 3, 2042; Charlotte (Charlie) Starborne" is what shows when the ink has dried.

Orson rests his hand on my shoulder as I tense. I'd like to contact his mother—I believe she forgot to teach him personal space. What a terrible example she must have been.

"Let's go. We have a case that came up this morning. Unless you'd rather start a fire somewhere." My face flushes and I clench my jaw to keep myself from slapping him. I'm not a violent person, but I wish I were. The only thing that stops me is the fear of the judge making my sentence longer. I stand down, and a few coworkers chuckle. *The joke of the precinct, that's what I am.*

Orson throws a glance at Honey, who is still watching us.

"Do you have something to say, Ms. Adler?" he scowls.

She quickly turns her attention to an officer. "Yes, Calliope, I will enter these files in the system."

The officer, who stands a half foot taller than Orson, has short-cut curly hair and light freckles. Her complexion is a rich brown, and she is wearing combat boots. I notice a flower in her hair. Honey sees the flower at the same time as me.

"Oh? Someone special, Calliope?" she asks.

The officer blushes. "A friend."

Honey smiles and Calliope rushes back to her station, papers overflowing the desk.

Orson leads me to the conference room, where a man who looks only a few years older than me sits, wearing the black-and-purple uniform of an officer. A new officer, fresh from training, I assume.

The stranger speaks first. "Mr. Bennet, is this the teenage intern you were talking about?" he says, smiling. I press my lips together, not breaking eye contact. He needs to feel all the hatred I have for him before he starts small talk. It's my only defense. God, the work I do defending myself at the precinct is draining.

"It's nice to meet you. My name is Luis, and you are . . . ?" He raises his eyebrows, awaiting a response.

"You seem eager." I'm wary to let him gather any information. Orson rolls his eyes, expecting the usual snappy comeback from me.

"The question is just a formality," Luis responds.

"This is Charlie, and she most certainly is not my intern. This chaotic delinquent committed a grave, and frankly, laughable offense, and the judge stuck her here for a year of community service. Luckily, her time with us is nearly over." He smirks, watching me. Orson is trying to get a rise out of me. It's cute, this juvenile banter, but I'm far more clever and not fueled by any respect for the man.

I remember our first meeting when he told me he was "older and therefore intellectually superior", insisting I call him by his last name. I refused, of course, because *Mr. Bennet* sounded like the spokesperson for a toothpaste commercial. I think our mutual hatred began at that moment, when I asked him if his teeth were shinier than his nose.

"Luis, is it? What an unfortunate name. If I were you, I'd sue your parents." Following my instincts, I sit in Orson's chair and prop my feet up on the table, taking note of Luis' posture and attitude. His short, brown hair is neatly combed back to show his striking blue eyes. Handsome, yet humble. Interesting. I notice that apart from when he addresses me, he never breaks eye contact with Orson, keeping his hands folded on the sleek wooden table.

To my surprise, the comment seems to not affect his mood. He doesn't even blink. That's it: he disgusts me.

Orson sits in the chair next to me, taking up my space, obtrusive and brutish. Luis starts lecturing on numbers or some other technical police work. I begin to drift off. Another day, another crime, nothing special about it. The guy gets caught, gets a trial, and is usually chucked in jail.

That could have been me. I discard the thought quicker than it appeared. Throughout the meeting, I am extra thoughtful to throw a sour expression at both Luis and Orson, refusing to let either one see my mind is elsewhere. Maintaining this default look serves its purpose—I get asked no questions the entire time.

Eventually, the boredom is too much to take. Pushing my palms against the desk, I slowly rise and watch with a slight smile as all eyes turn to me. "I think we're done here." I hiss, brushing my hair out of my face. I grab the silver elastic hairband around my wrist, using it to pull my hair back and keep it in place. Orson shakes his head, tightening his lips. He couldn't stop me if he wanted to. But Luis is new and ambitious. He walks up to me, believing he can persuade me with reason. I hold up a hand, and to my pleasant surprise, he stops. *Weak.*

"I believe you're missing something."

Luis checks his pockets. "My . . . wallet? Where's my wallet?"

"Not bad for a delinquent, eh?"

The wallet makes a *thump* as I drop it on the conference table. Luis' eyes grow wide, fixing his gaze on me. He continues to stare as I make my way out of the conference room.

"I told you, we'll need her," I hear Orson say.

"You're right. This one's a keeper," Luis replies.

What a waste of breath. They "need me." Sure, let them try to use me for whatever case they have planned. I can do whatever I want. I could move to New Mexico if it suited me. They can't stop . . .

My face falls.

I'm trapped here, where the city can keep tabs on me. This place gets some excitement, but other than that it's a silent desert, and I'm a cactus that stays planted to one spot. Destined to live in this cage until I die and eventually decompose. Yet another beautiful simile, but I don't write this one down. *What a dismal way to start the day.* I need to escape.

CHAPTER 2

"Charlie? Is that you?" I hear my mom calling from the kitchen as my full bookbag drops to the floor. After the meeting, Luis caught up to me, saying it would benefit me to read up on government and law. As he went on about things like pie charts and arrests, all I could think about was going home to my mom. She is the only person who was proud enough of me to stay after finding out I could be a troublemaker. I slide my house key into my back pocket. *Safe.*

I walk into the steamy kitchen to find my mom pulling a tin of meatloaf out of the oven. She wipes the sweat from her brow, her black hair cut short to stay out of the way of the food. Three home-cooked meals a day never gets old.

Let me say a few words about Ivy Starborne:

My mom is a minimalistic yet complex person, like me. That's why I appreciate her. She'd rather have the simple things. She doesn't need the long, luscious locks of hair that most girls defend with their lives. I glance down at the curls of my own hair. Am I the same as the girls I swear to detest? No. I'll cut it to match my mom's. Just not today.

"Charlotte, I made meatloaf and peas for dinner tonight," she says, pouring a whopping spoonful of peas onto my platter. Not many people today see the appeal in home-cooked meals. Why spend hours standing in front of a steaming oven when you could order food to be flown to your house by drone? Yet another reason to love my mom: she's always the first to go against the grain. To speak up against all odds, especially when she knows she's right.

She works from home, as do most people I know. There's not much point in going to an office when you can do all the work on a digital cube or in a digitized workroom. It allows a family to be together. Many instead use the opportunity to become hermits, never leaving the house and only blinking when their eyes are about to dry out.

A smile from my mother snaps me back into the moment. Her smiles are always genuine. You can tell she means it. I slump into the stiff, familiar chair of my home. Mom found a set of rustic wooden furniture online and I didn't complain. She said they made the kitchen more "homey" than the usual pick of cushioned plastic or metal.

She was right. I can finally relax.

"How are your grades?" My head perks up at this question. She quizzes me about my day, the questions always coming at me in rapid-fire succession. It makes me feel more awake and in the moment. I guess it helps you to realize that your school day wasn't completely wasted. When I tally up the classes and assignments, I feel so much more productive.

"I'm making good grades," I answer simply. "My mentors at school all tell me I should be taking a more accelerated course." My mom nods, scooping a spoonful of peas into her mouth.

"And everything is okay at school? No . . . *disruptions?*" She eyes me carefully.

I shake my head. "I haven't seen him, don't worry."

I'm about to change the subject when the lights flicker above my head, signaling me to answer the doorbell. My dad was partly deaf, so we installed the light system when he lived here. Glancing at my full plate, I go to answer the door.

The screen next to the door shows a girl with pale skin and a braid of honey-colored hair standing at the door. She shows the confidence of a toothpick. I press a button and the door slides into the wall. The girl jumps and adjusts her glasses. Who is she trying to impress?

I decide I can have fun with this, pressing my arm against the doorframe. She watches me, wide-eyed. A girl from my school, I assume. I don't pay much attention to the people there. Few have the potential to go anywhere and many who do, fall into the trap of laziness. They're all mindless sheep in a herd, only entertained by each other. It's not worth it to talk to a sheep.

"Did you have something to say?" I say. She stays silent. The girl looks a little older than me.

This was fun for a second or two. Now her shyness is just plain annoying. I decide to take a leap. "Would you like to come in?" I step to the side. She says nothing as she enters. I analyze her from head to toe as I close the door.

"I guess my first question would be your name. My family doesn't get many visitors," I say.

A simple, unintelligible mumble comes from her lips.

"I'm sorry, what was that?" I step closer, raising an eyebrow.

"I believe she said 'Bree.'" My mom hums, stepping out from the kitchen and wiping her hands on her jeans. "Nice to meet you, Bree. You can call me Ivy. That's more of a privilege than my daughter gets. She has to call me 'mom'. Can I get you anything?"

Bree shakes her head, looking between me and my mom. It seems she's playing a game of *Spot the Difference: Mother-Daughter Edition*. I grab Bree's arm, dragging her upstairs before my mom can suggest she stay for dinner or a sleepover. A *sleepover* was a term used in my mom's time. It means that a person would stay the night at a friend's house. What's the point of going over to someone's house only to sleep in the same room?

Bree looks traumatized. I can only imagine what she could be thinking. She knocks on a stranger's door only to be kidnapped by the people inside. Poor girl. Except I couldn't care less. She interrupted my time with my mom, and there are two things I cherish: my time and my family. The only thing that stopped me from shutting the door in her face was the potential for adventure. Maybe a story to share for an easy A on a school project.

I walk into my room, Bree following close behind. She stops at the door upon seeing my messy room. I glance around, thinking back to all the times I've mindlessly tossed clothes and objects around the room.

"I *told* you we rarely get guests." I poke the side of my digital cube, type in a code, and a small bot appears to clean any dirty spots with carpet soap or a vacuum. Bree watches, her eyes shooting around, catching every detail. The drawer that holds my shirts, the nightstand where my page-reader is set, and the windowsill that holds my portable self-filtering water bottle. I watch her absorbing every small detail, grasping for intel in every corner. She catches my stare, quickly blushing and looking away.

"I guess you're not around technology that often, huh? Are your family a bunch of relics?" I say.

"Is that what you call them? My family listens to a CD every now and then and likes to read books made from paper, but that doesn't necessarily mean—"

"You still haven't told me why you're here," I remind her, tapping my fingers on the decorative chrome desk next to the door.

"O-oh. Right. I'm here to tell you that I was sent by Mr. Bennet," she says, gripping a chair in the room as if she might faint at any moment.

I run a hand through my hair, not saying anything. Bree watches, wiping her hands on her shirt. I walk over, leaning close to her face. Her breath smells like fresh strawberries. I notice that her eyes are a strong green, contrasting with her apparent personality. There's something else there, and I'm not sure I want to trust it yet.

"Tell Orson that whatever he wants, he's not getting it. I have four weeks before I leave the precinct, and he's not going to ruin them," I growl.

Bree shrinks back, like a mouse retreating into its hole. I stare her down, but in a sudden rush of adrenaline, she speaks up.

"Mr. Bennet wants you back at the precinct. Something important came up," Bree manages to say.

I search her eyes for anything suspicious behind them but find nothing. This girl is too innocent to be living in this city. "What does this have to do with you, exactly? I've never seen you before. Bennet could have come here himself or called."

"It was too risky. This is something classified." Bree speaks as if she's an agent for the government, yet the sweet undertone to her voice ruins it. Why is she being trusted with this "top-secret" information? Why have I never seen her before? What did this have to do with me?

I relent. "Fine. I'll go. Are we walking?"

"Officer Fysher is waiting outside for us in his car," she responds, starting to walk out. The name rings a bell. I think for a moment before stopping in my tracks.

"I get to go on an adventure with Ms. Goody-Two-Shoes and handsome Luis Fysher?" I hint at a smile, not wanting to show my uncertainty about this vague situation. What could Bree, Luis, and especially Orson, want from me? I've been called a "delinquent" for over a year now at the precinct, but now they want to trust me with government-protected information? It must be a trick.

I feel the cool summer breeze as I step outside. My mom has most likely washed the dishes by now and left the kitchen to finish up some work. She must think I'm still in my room. There's no need to tell her that I'm leaving. She'll worry.

Bree gets in the waiting black-and-purple police hovercar, looking at me. I bite the inside of my cheek as I climb into the vehicle, nearly jumping out of my socks when I see Luis reclining in a seat, a small stack of papers in his hand, staring like he'd been expecting us for hours.

I scan the layout of the car's interior, noting four seats facing one another that make the car into a moving common space. I don't usually travel by car. They're useless, according to me and my mom. We can walk to the places we need to be. I believe that exercise is necessary, especially after seeing how lazy and privileged the kids at my school are, letting cars and trains carry them to their destinations like royalty.

Luis and Bree both stare at me.

"A little too interested, aren't you?" I glare at them.

"No, not at all. I think you're just as boring as you feel I am," Luis says, chuckling. I make a fist, ready to punch him, when the seatbelt buckles for me. I look down at the plastic strap across my torso, trying to unbuckle it.

Bree giggles. "It's a police car, Charlie. The officers in the car have to be secure."

I'm about to ask a question before pounding anger hits me in the form of a slight headache.

I grit my teeth. She knows my name, but I never introduced myself. It's enough to set off red flags.

Luis smiles, reading my face. "We know all about you, Charlotte. I've known about you since before we met. We have much to discuss. Let's head to the precinct."

I still feel ready to fight before the exhaustion hits me. Instead, I lean back and watch the leaves dance in the May wind as the car whisks by.

CHAPTER 3

The car's motion has nearly rocked me to sleep by the time we arrive at the precinct. I snap awake, looking around the hovercar as the past hour comes back to me. Luis presses a button on the roof of the car, allowing our seatbelts to retract back into the seats. The three of us climb out. I shiver, focusing on the dark, dreary building ahead to distract me from the cold air.

Something unexpected catches my attention: the sky. I don't get out much at night because I'm rarely trusted to leave the house except for my community service sentence or school.

I can't believe my eyes. The dark, vast atmosphere seems to be alive. It's as if someone has bedazzled the empty space with jewels and sequins, all glittering in silence. A band of clustered stars shines in my face. The Milky Way. When the citizens are asleep, the sky is wide awake. It seems like a good balance. How can a person spend their entire life without looking up?

"Never seen the sky at night? Don't worry, you're part of the majority." Luis stands next to me, his eyes glimmering as they look at the sky, just as mine do.

"How—"

"The International Pollution Act of 2030," Bree interrupts. "Every country in the world was required to create more eco-friendly environments. Less plastic, a decrease in factories, and a greater need for multipurpose devices. Not to mention the replacement of eighty-five percent of electric energy lighting. The world primarily uses stored solar power for artificial lighting purposes." She smiles, rocking back and forth on her heels. Too proud of her useless knowledge. I glare, and Bree immediately looks away.

I remember why I was brought here and storm into the dark building. The doors slide away at my approach. I can feel the eyes of Luis and Bree burning into the back of my head, hearing their footprints close behind me.

"Time is a thief, Charlie! Hurry up!" Orson yells. I can see him behind the clear walls of the conference room. I walk in, returning his smug expression. I sit in a chair, spinning until it's hard to tell the difference between the walls and the floor. Luis grabs the back of the seat to stop it.

"This is serious. You might want to listen to what we have to say," Luis says, sitting next to me. Bree comfortably leans against the wall near the door, and this suddenly feels like an intervention. I haven't done anything. Maybe the situation is all a misunderstanding. I get ready to stand but halt when Orson speaks.

"I assume you're wondering why you're here—"

"I didn't do anything wrong. You can't send me back to the judge.

I'd like to see proof," I say, standing and making for the door. Bree steps in front of me. I could fight her, and we both know she would lose.

"Charlotte, it's okay. We're here because we need your help," she says in a calming tone. I'm not falling for it.

"And who are you, exactly? Why has no one explained anything? If you people know what's good for you, you'll start talking before someone gets hurt." My eyes narrow.

Out of the corner of my eye, I see Luis approaching. I glare at each of the three bodies in the room, knowing that I can fight my way out, but afraid of the consequences. I know what I am now. All bark, no bite. It's a clear sign of desperation.

"Give us a chance to explain everything, Ms. Starborne. You'll understand in a minute." Luis pulls my chair back, motioning me to sit back down. Adrenaline still coursing through my veins, I sit on the edge of the seat, ready to jump up at any time. The others find their way back to their chairs, and I can see that these people are different from my normal mentors and classmates at school. Bree and Luis carry themselves differently than the average person, as if they have something more important going on with their lives. I recognize it as the confidence that I pretend I have. I lean back in my seat comfortably, though I'm far from it.

"Now that everyone's calmed down," Orson says, throwing a glance at me, "we can finally get to business." I grit my teeth at his remark but say nothing. Numerous unpleasant retorts circle in my mind as Orson leans on his knuckles on the table. A man who refuses to show any vulnerability, always searching for a new power move. A small grin creeps across his face as he dangles the growing suspense in the air.

He places a digital cube in front of him, pressing the side. The cube flickers a few times, then casts a hologram in front of us. Orson steps to the side, and I squint at the image, trying to understand the lines of code presented in front of me. Bree rises to stand opposite Orson, reminding me of the annoying class presentations at school.

"Charlie, let me introduce you to our 'EASY' program, or 'Episodic Analyzing of Suspects: Code Yellow.'" Bree says this as if it were as simple as teaching a five-year-old how to work a hovercar. I manage to keep my face expressionless. I feel all the eyes around the room burning into my skin. "Now, I realize that you're probably confused, as most would be, but the program is actually quite simple," the unusual teenager continues, and I tense. I don't like being patronized.

"This program will revolutionize the criminal investigation world forever. No more useless interrogations that can lead cops to a dead end." Her words are certain, showing forethought—I can tell she's done this before. Each word has a certain passion to it. "After years of careful programming, we've nearly perfected it, and it's ready to be tested in the real world. The suspect walks into the interrogation room and drinks a vial of liquid that will make them relive the event that has happened. Then, from the other side of the double glass, the police can witness exactly what happened from the suspect's point of view on a screen. This revolutionary liquid contains a nanochip that the brain recognizes and sends messages to, projecting the exact scenes from a crime onto a monitor. Afterward, the suspect forgets that they have relived the event. A suspect cannot withhold information or lie. It is a foolproof way for an officer to solve crimes as fast and as accurately as possible."

My brain maps out the information as Bree draws the foundation and walls for me. I blink a few times, but not because I don't understand. "Wait," I say, processing this new information and quickly scanning through the endless lists of code on the hologram in front of me. "So, your program . . . looks through a person's memory and plays it on a monitor for police officers to watch?"

"Exactly," Luis pitches in, speaking in a casual, encouraging tone. I stare at Orson, Bree, and Luis, speechless.

"Something wrong?" Bree says. They look concerned, or at least Luis and Bree do.

"This all seems a little . . . immoral," I say.

"It'll help millions." Bree smiles. "Investigations will take almost no time, and no innocent will ever be incarcerated by accident again. Besides, the government has already approved it. The 'Code Yellow' means that they were a little on the fence about it, but they still gave us the go-ahead on our project. What's one person's memory when you could save hundreds?"

I glance at Orson, who has been as quiet as a shadow, and remember where I am.

"Who are you people? I think by now I should have gotten that explanation," I say, watching their unchanging expressions. Luis sees an opportunity to jump in, standing at the head of the table between Orson and Bree. Orson grabs the digital cube, and it shuts off the hologram so all I can see are the three of them watching me.

I notice how peculiar the team looks together, their ages and looks clashing like green, purple, and maroon. Luis is the tallest and carries himself with pride. Orson is shorter than Luis but much taller than Bree. He always wears a serious expression. Bree is short and fidgety, yet anyone who takes a second look at her could see that her mind is always at work. The train of my observations stops when Luis speaks in his loud, but kind, voice. A born leader.

"We all work with the Justice Division within the federal government, Charlotte. We began our work with Officer Calliope a year ago, but she had to bow out due to a bigger case. That was around the time you came in. You could say we've been watching you for a while. The Justice Division feels that you can help us with our program. EASY needs a lot of teamwork, and we need an action crew. Bree here is the brains of the operation. She planned and coded the program. The department took her in to work for them, and now she's here with our project."

"The government? What is this?" I say. I have many more questions, but it seems like this initiation ceremony has a limit on curiosity.

"Let me explain. I was in my office one day, working as a police cadet, and doing paperwork on computers. My job was to review filed police reports, one by one. Hour after long hour. After a while, I realized how useless it was. Years of police training, just to end up working a desk job, making an unfulfilling salary. That was when I came up with the idea for EASY and put Bree on the project to code."

"I had no idea how to make it work," Bree says, "until Orson and I were talking one day, and he mentioned a potential suspect for a new case. The owner of a multibillion-dollar company that links technology to the human brain, allowing a person's mind to control the device's action. By reversing the relationship between brainwaves and electrodes, the EASY program can direct and organize memory."

Luis nods. "Exactly. After months of development, we received orders to transfer to this city and work with Orson. All we need now is eyes and ears on the ground. Someone who isn't afraid to get their hands dirty."

I realize now why they turned to me: a one-time criminal who is expendable enough to send on missions.

I toss the idea around in my mind. Being a spy for the government sounds like fun, so it couldn't hurt to try. Plus, I have a little time left with the precinct until my sentence is over.

A slow grin spreads across my face. I look at the three waiting for my answer.

"I'll do it."

CHAPTER 4

It's official: I hate Luis.

Not that he was "all that and a bag of dried watermelon chips" before, but I said I'd join the team. I didn't agree to this workload.

Sitting on the floor of my room, I flip through the pages of *The '20s: A Government Restructured*. I'd rather stick my head in a trash compactor than read this drivel. My clock reads 3:55 a.m. and I'm still on page twelve. Not that there's any point to getting past Chapter 1. It's all "population decrease" and "riots" and "the entire rearrangement of the government's structure." I'm top of Mrs. Garby's History and Politics class. I could recite this stuff in my sleep.

But it's looking like I'll never *get* to sleep. It's a Saturday, so I would typically have a half-day at school starting at noon, but Luis wants me at the precinct, at 6:30 sharp, to go over the material I've learned. I don't really see the point, but hey, *he's the boss.*

I nearly snap the pencil I'm holding.

At 6:00 a.m. I shove my stupid books into my stupid bag and leave for my quiz with stupid Luis. Before stepping out of the door, I take a breath. *I* am working on a government project, and *I* have to act a little more mature than I have been this morning. I will be on time, do whatever is asked, and get through my sentence so I can get out of here.

Still, no promises.

When I get to the precinct, it's empty aside from a stream of light coming from the conference room. Luis is standing at the end of the conference table, a digital cube casting a hologram. The text is backward from my view, but it looks like an article.

"Take your seat," he says.

I sit at the other end of the table, toss my book bag onto the ground, and cross my arms. "Okay, *Mr. Fysher*. Do I at least get a class syllabus?"

He glances over and turns the screen off. "I'm sorry?"

There goes my chance at Government Project Assistant of the Month.

"Charlie," he says, and shuffles some papers around, "do you know why I asked you to come here today?"

"Enlighten me."

Luis pauses and looks at the wall above me. "I'd like to see if you can figure it out. Why don't we begin?"

"All right, fine. Where's the link to the test?" I reach for the digital cube in my bag.

"No link. You will tell me your answers directly."

I stare. I was hoping to speed through this exam and be out of here in ten minutes.

"Why do you always insist on doing things the old-fashioned way?

Why does everyone here? Paper books, printed diagrams, tests that aren't online?"

He folds his hands behind his back. "Maybe I'm sentimental that way. Or maybe, if you'd read the book, you would know that online work isn't as socially gratifying."

My nose wrinkles. Luis is implying that I didn't do my homework. I didn't, but it's still offensive.

The test begins.

If there's some deeper meaning to whatever this is, I'll have to note the questions' patterns. Before I can think up a snarky answer, he asks the first question.

Essentially, it's about the contrast in teenagers now versus teenagers in the '20s. I fiddle with the sleeve of my jacket because I now have to compare myself to my mom in high school. Yeah . . . Mrs. Garby never covered this one. I was expecting an election question, or something about the global shutdown, or the crazy virus thing.

After a while, a flicker of amusement passes through Luis' eyes. "Would you like me to 'enlighten you?'"

"Is this some type of pop culture quiz?"

"I wanted to see if you'd read past the first two chapters. Clearly, you haven't. So, we're going to shake things up a bit. I'm going to teach you."

"Oh, God. This wasn't your plan all along, was it?"

"It was my backup. Let's begin with the third wave of the Great Pandemic, which wiped out 23 percent of the earth's population . . ."

This time, I don't dissociate from the conversation. It's kind of nostalgic to think about my mom's life before I was born.

Luis explains that as the virus of the '20s became more dangerous, my mom's generation began to speak out. Expectations for minors rose, then came the explosion of '25.

Not an actual explosion. The pandemic caused a massive population decrease, which in turn made the economy decline and led to another government shutdown. That happened right before I was born.

The country turned to teens to make up for what was lost. Federal legislation threw young adults' high expectations into action. One law made the drinking age 18, accelerated all education, and gave teens the right to work full-time, anywhere, at the age of thirteen, with the same benefits and salary as someone three times their age.

It took a while to enforce nationally, but it became the norm within a few years. The early '20s had already twisted life, so why wouldn't people try something new? I don't remember the way life was before, and from what I read, I'm not sure I'd want to.

"Charlie, the education you're getting now is the education of a junior at a university in the 2010s. It's why I started a career at fifteen. That's the only reason why you're not living in a dumpster right now and why I have a degree."

"And you're telling me this . . . why?"

Luis sighs. "I want you to understand what we're doing and why we're doing it." He turns the hologram on again and spins the digital cube so the text is facing me. The article from earlier is now showing a graph titled "CRIME RATES, 2015-Present." The green line on the graph increases exponentially up to 2039, decreases by a small margin up to 2042, then stops at a black dot.

"*This*," he motions to the graph, "is where we come in. Because when kids and teens were forced to accelerate their growth to get the economy and our society back to what it was, the crime rate—"

"Blew up like a marshmallow in the microwave?" I give myself a mental high-five for that one.

"Precisely. This isn't only due to teens, though. There are far worse evils out there that we have to deal with." Luis smiles a bit. I think he's proud to get through to me. I won't let him hold onto that victory for long. "The Justice Division was then created to manage that crime rate in a more creative and proactive way. We want fewer officers out in the field and more working with technology. It's safer and more efficient. There are projects like EASY across the country. It's a competition to see who can fix the world."

"And *why* are you making this sound like a derby?"

"Because," the pride on his face shatters, "I want you to *understand*. I want you to be *passionate*. Please, I am giving you homework to prepare you for work with us in the future—"

My pride shatters as well. The walls are back up.

"You're not serious, are you?" I say. "There will be no future with this team. I will do your cutesy little spy work, end my time with the precinct, and you will never hear from me again."

"Charlotte—"

"'Fix the world,'" I scoff and walk out of the conference room, leaving the bag of books behind. Like he or I or anyone else could make an ounce of a difference. What a waste of time.

Still, the adrenaline rushes through me. I could be wrong.

Wow, I never thought I'd think those words. But we'll just have to see.

CHAPTER 5

A person can have many positive attributes. A kind heart, a sharp mind, a strong will. But more often than not, a person's faults will shine through like a ray of light through a cracked shutter. Every so often, you can use those weaknesses to accentuate your strengths.

Last night and this morning replay in my head as I get ready for school. My first mission starts today, and I can feel the blood coursing through my veins. All I need to do is remember the strength of my faults and keep the oxygen flowing to my brain.

I decide to skip breakfast and toss a quick "love you" to my mom as I head to school. Jumping the fence, as usual, I land on my feet and kick up the dust beneath me. The city is more alive now. Bullet trains whoosh past, taking people where they need to go. I approach the modern-looking glass exterior of the high school.

My peers walk through the halls, talking and joking around, and I watch from the outside, looking in. The windows keep every student on display, so no secrets are hidden. But the clear walls also keep us at a distance from the world. I step through the weapons detector in the door, getting a green light to enter.

A sweet voice breaks the chatters of the scattered crowd, announcing that it is 9:15; time to go to our classes. Some kids throw phrases like "see ya!" and "meet you at lunch!" to their friends across the hall before retreating into their separate worlds. I take a moment to let the pathway clear. It doesn't take long before my peers are in class and only a few rogue teens are rushing to beat the tardy announcement. I lean against a glass pane, tossing my digital cube between my palms. It's time for my favorite game of the day.

I check the time on the clock on the ceiling. It's 9:18. I wait until the clock flashes 9:19, then break into a sprint across the building. With the hallway devoid of foot traffic, the floor is mine. I feel the adrenaline pumping like a ticking clock. Sixty seconds to make it across the building. I glance at the clock on the next floor. Still 9:19. The first class of the day comes into sight, and I slow the pace, knowing I've beaten the bell.

My stride settles into a walk before I reach the room. The door slides open at my approach, and eyes fall to me as the *ding* of the bell for class to start rings. I straighten my spine and walk to my seat, making eye contact with anyone who dares. Front row, closest to the exit. It's the most practical seat in the room. My mentor, Mr. Ariosto, clears his throat, smiling at me. The holo-screens flicker in front of us as we start our lesson, and my mind leaves my body as I start to work.

I enjoy Mr. Ariosto's class, but I cannot stand the students. Relics who sit in the back of the class, refusing to pay a lick of attention, and playing catch with their holo-screen styluses. One kid brags about his new tablet computer and another shows off her phone, complete with games and entertainment platforms. Most deemed phone applications a waste of time years ago when the world was working to rebuild. Still, some with money get the luxury of laziness in their teen years.

I quickly finish the assignment and turn my holo-screen off to leave. As the screen disappears, I hear the last of Mr. Ariosto's lecture. He speaks with passion and surety.

"—from great philosophers, such as Aristotle and Socrates, we learn that nothing is black and white. Everything and anything can have meaning, especially when you do not mean it to. A simple phrase can mean one million things to one million people. It can mean nothing, and something, all at the same time. When man is faced with the danger of a question, he can be afraid, but it is impossible to come up with the wrong answer in a realm of endless points of view."

His words should seem pointless to me, but I feel that it is the simple answer I needed. I've thought of tonight's mission as unethical, but is it really? If there are no wrong answers, I have no reason to fear succeeding with what *I feel* is an immoral action.

I have been taught to try to do what is right, so I can go on with my mission now, knowing that I will help a person who cannot help themself. What my mentor said is true. A seemingly uncomplicated phrase can mean one million things to one million people, so my mission tonight could be seen as ethical and fair to nearly anyone. I relax, feeling more ready than ever before.

The rest of the day is more or less a blur, with mentors and peers acting as if they know the world best. Mr. Ariosto's humble words play over and over in my mind, like a broken hologram. What's the point of life if you can't live it in the right way? My decisions can never be good enough if someone else will see my actions as a bad deed. Maybe the important thing is doing what you *feel* is right. Maybe my psychology mentor has a point as sharp as a needle, and I had completely missed it. Maybe—

A loud *ding* rings through the school, signaling us to head home. For me, it's my cue for another day's work at the precinct. I let out a relieved sigh. It's better to focus on what's important rather than following a rabbit trail. It's time to stop the senseless questioning and leave.

Preparing for the long walk to the police station, I take a small container out of my back pocket, removing a neon orange pill from it. "EarthKey," I mumble, reading the side of the container. The pill dissolves in my mouth as I walk, connecting to my digital cube and the playlist of music I want. The capsule, now in my system, will allow me to not only listen but feel the music as I walk. No pesky cords or accessories are needed.

I bob my head nonchalantly, stepping into the precinct. A new air fills the atmosphere. A feeling of contentment that a year of serving time couldn't accomplish. As if I am finally getting somewhere. Ms. Adler's eyebrows rise in my presence, happiness radiating from her face. I don't return the expression, and sign "May 4, 2042; Charlotte (Charlie) Starborne" on the sheet at the desk then make my way past her checkpoint.

Luis, Bree, and Orson are already in the conference room, discussing things beyond my expertise. I turn a chair around to lean into it sideways and will my EarthKey to pause the playlist.

"Don't you people have better things to do with your lives than stay cooped up in this room all day?" I ask.

"We're doing important work here, Charlotte," Orson snarls. "But of course a child would have trouble understanding."

We share a glance of hatred before Luis takes his place at the front of the table. Bree evens out a stack of papers, and I examine them quickly, hoping to get some insight into the plan. It's digits and symbols. *Great.* She tentatively watches Luis, ignoring my interest in her work. Or maybe she wants me to notice and is letting me follow my curiosity. I return my attention to Luis.

"We begin in an hour, where our sources tell us our . . . ironically unsuspecting suspect will be at an uptown bar called Busy Tuxedo, a formal establishment that serves the upscale market. Charlie—" I look up, "—we've bought you a dress fit for the occasion, as well as acquired an ID and a VIP pass to make it through the door. We'll feed you details through the earpiece you'll be wearing. After you lure the suspect into your provided limo, you will knock him out with a drugged beverage, and he'll wake up in our investigation room. Bree will be running the EASY program from behind the two-way glass, while Orson gives our suspect the vial."

I process the instructions slowly, nodding. "What will you be doing?" I cross my arms, analyzing the room's atmosphere.

"Operating everything in the background. So, what do you say, Starborne? Are you in for a little adventure?" His eyes dare me to think through my next response, and I tighten my lips. I can't say no to a little danger; after all, this is the type of thing all senseless adrenaline junkies dream of. Luckily, I'm not so senseless. I've learned from my sentence here that it can benefit me to listen. But it wouldn't hurt to have a little fun.

My eyes dart back at Luis, and I nod. He understands and slides a suspect file over to me. The team is called into action, and I can feel the tension I've held in for a year leave me.

CHAPTER 6

The Busy Tuxedo. The name fits. The outside of the bar is crowded with men and women, most in suits and dresses that I can't afford, trying to beg their way through the door. I roll my eyes and ignore them. It's just like school. *These people are inferior to you. You have more important things to attend to.*

My rose-colored heels click on the pavement as I walk through small groups looking for a bar at which to spend their night, and my gaze never falters from the door. I stand straighter than I usually would, looking up at the bouncer who is between me and the finish line—the big, sliding door to the inside.

His glance shifts to me, and I smile politely, taking my fake ID and VIP permit out of the handbag I'm holding. I notice the color matches my shoes. *Nice job, Luis. I guess men aren't all tasteless.* The bouncer scans the VIP card onto the scanner he's holding, and it blinks green. He nods back at me and presses a button on his wristband. The door welcomes me. I'm in.

The first thing that hits me as I step inside is the colorful smell of alcohol mixing in the air. A blended aroma of both bitter and sweet, coming together perfectly. I've never tried alcohol, but it couldn't hurt. Especially for an Orson-run mission. The second thing I notice is that I have to squint to see the dance floor. The lights flow through each other rapidly, moving to a beat that I can't hear.

All bars now are silent. You need to buy an EarthKey pill at a certain table in order to hear anything. That way you can personalize your music. They're all DJs' picks, but you can choose the volume, the key, and more. Without an EarthKey, all you hear is the mumbling, laughing, and squeaking of shoes around you. It's pretty ingenious, if you ask me. Speaking of innovations . . ..

"Luis? Hello?" I say to the air and hope I'm using my earpiece right. Just a girl, standing on a dance floor, speaking to herself. *Charlie Starborne, a real hero.* After getting no response, I begin to stalk around, looking for my target. Back at the precinct, the three of them are probably waiting for me to make a move. Observing me like a lab rat. I wonder which of my actions would make Orson the angriest and decide to try a drink.

I slide into a chair, twirling my hair with my finger. The bartender is with a customer right now. I won't bother him. Before long, an older man, probably in his fifties, sits down next to me. Deciding this half-drunken man isn't worth my time, I turn my head the other way, ignoring him.

"I love your dress," he says. I glance over. His toothy grin doesn't reach his eyes. I understand that he's expecting a response, but it's safer to deny his existence. It's not time for games, even if it does sound fun to mess with a guy who won't remember my face the next morning.

After noticing my inattentiveness, he waves the bartender over. I hear him ordering a beer, and something called a Tequila Sunrise. I hope he's not going to drink both. The last thing I need on my mission is a drunken fifty-two-year-old following me around like a duckling.

To my surprise, the bartender sets one of the two drinks directly in front of me. I know what a beer looks like, so I assume this fruity beverage is the Tequila Sunrise.

A woman on my left, who I didn't even notice sit down, lightly elbows me. Her raspy voice speaks of experience. "Honey, if you get a free drink, drink it. I see your bug eyes. Taking a drink isn't accepting a proposal. Just make sure it's the bartender who gives it to you, then get up and go when you're done. No strings attached."

She winks at me, and I look back to the man, who is already on his second mug of beer. I look back to my drink, alive with colors of orange and red, and bring the glass up to my lips. I raise my eyebrows, catching a citrusy taste that I would have never expected. This seems like just the thing to wake me up. The drink is gone in a matter of minutes, and I start to search for the bartender before a voice makes me halt in my tracks.

"Not so fast, Starborne. You're on duty," Orson remarks through the buzzing earpiece. "We can't have a drunk agent, now, can we? Stay on task. The target has yet to arrive."

"Killjoy," I mumble, forgetting again that Bree, Orson, and Luis can hear every word I say. But it doesn't matter. I'm feeling more rebellious than I've felt in a while. A little adrenaline —and alcohol— coursing through your blood never hurt anyone. It's too much heart-pumping that can kill you.

"Our tracker says that he should be arriving any second," Bree says. I can picture her now: her nose in a screen, her big brain solving puzzles that don't yet exist. The door slides open and, just as predicted, a man with bright green eyes that complement his square face enters. He's wearing a suit that screams *I could buy this bar* and looks around the room with a certainty I could never understand.

"That's our guy," Luis says, and I can hear the focus in his voice. He's probably already planning four steps ahead. I must seem like a childish little girl to this team of superstars.

I'll show them. I glide over to the man, taking a card out of Bree's playbook. Act too shy for anyone to suspect your deception.

I fold my hands in front of me, bending my head slightly to look up at him through the ends of my eyelashes. I start out using a meek voice. A bunny in a den of wolves. "Hello, I'm so sorry, but I noticed you from across the room, and you just stood out to me. I mustered up the courage to talk to you," I let out a small giggle, "but if you're here on important business, I can come back at a better time." *Jesus, I wish they had classes in flirtation at school.*

He watches me, a smile growing on his face. This doesn't seem like a man to commit a felony, but sometimes the most seemingly trustworthy people can turn out to be the worst of all. I maintain my shy appearance, gathering any information I can from looking at him. I'm wearing an eyepiece that sends everything I see back to the precinct so they can look up his files.

"Joseph," he says.

"I know many Josephs. You'll have to do better than that, 'just Joseph,'" I reply.

"You're right. Terribly sorry. Joseph Foster. And yours?" He holds out his hand. I shake it, taking the extra time to come up with a fake name.

"Mable Sinclair." I mentally pat myself on the back for the quick thinking, and I can hear Orson's distant chuckles from the earpiece. Joseph's eyes track mine, and I look back at him.

"You're wearing a lovely dress."

This time, the compliment catches me. I guess that's because I'm receiving it from a handsome gentleman and not a drunkard. I look down at my dress.

It's a light pink party dress, short enough for dancing. The lace sleeves fall to my wrists, and a beautiful flower pattern runs from the top to the waist, where the skirt flows out in an array of silk. What I love most is the gemstone belt around my stomach. When Luis and Bree presented the outfit to me, my heart jumped.

Before today, I would have never even considered wearing such a masterpiece, but when I looked at myself in the mirror after Bree zipped the top, I didn't see *Charlie Starborne, Teenage Punk* written across my forehead. I saw *Charlotte*. I saw a new start. Since that moment, I've been considering staying in the Justice Department after my sentence is over.

Joseph intervenes in my thought process.

"We are at a bar, are we not? Let's have a drink, Mable," he says, grinning. I try to hide my smirk. This is just too easy. I was hoping this mission wouldn't take too long, and it seems the first step is almost complete.

"You're right. But I was actually hoping we wouldn't have to sit at that dusty bar." I play with a lock of my hair.

"Oh? What else did you have in mind?"

"I have a limo waiting for us at the curb."

His eyebrow raises, and I release a small smile, offering my hand.

"A limo? Mable Sinclair, you're more mysterious than I first imagined."

"Let's just say I have connections. Why not," I pause, searching for the right phrase, "take a leap of faith? I find searching for answers often leads to finding them."

"I might prefer the dusty bar."

I bite the inside of my cheek. "I didn't take you as a quitter, playing it safe."

"Oh? I can assure you I don't typically play it safe."

"Then prove it."

Joseph looks down at my hand and takes it. We walk out of the silent bar and back into the chaos outside. The crowd is still here, offering bribes and more to the bouncer as he turns each person away. I look around, not seeing a vehicle.

"It's around the corner. I thought you'd enjoy a brief stroll," Luis' voice buzzes through the earpiece.

"Jerk," I mumble.

"What was that?" Joseph says.

"Hm? Oh, nothing. My vehicle is this way."

I lead Joseph to the side of the building. A hovering white limo waits for us, the door hissing open. I climb in after our suspect and press a button for the door to close. He is sealed in.

Before Joseph notices, I quickly examine the space, noticing a small bar built into the car's interior.

"So, champagne or white wine?" I say, taking two glasses from the minibar. Before he can reply, I start pouring champagne into both containers. It'll be easier to dissolve a pill in this drink. I wait until Joseph's attention is on his watch, then drop a tablet into the drink closest to him. He watches the city out of the window, and I wonder what life looks like through his eyes. A man about to be taken to a precinct where he will be interrogated for a crime. How can a man, who has done something so wrong that it would make the police suspect him of a felony, be so calm at a time like this?

I look out of the window for a few moments, watching pedestrians in shimmering dresses make their way to the club.

Joseph clears his throat and picks up one of the glasses. I take the other and sip the champagne. I've tried alcohol twice in one day now. That's something to check off the Bucket List.

"Anything you'd like to say? A mini-toast?" I ask. He considers this for a moment.

"To getting what we want," he smiles, raising his glass. I do the same.

"I'll drink to that, Joseph Foster."

"As will I, Mable Sinclair."

His words have a new edge to them, and I make sure to note this before we both down the rest of our drinks. The next few moments are silent. We both watch each other.

"How are you feeling? You look a bit red," Joseph says.

"I'm feeling all right. How about you?" I say back.

Joseph's mouth moves, but gibberish comes out of his mouth. I squint to pretend I understand but become distracted by my slowed breathing. Trying hard to keep control, I tell my arms to move but notice I'm on the ground, although I never felt myself falling. Joseph speaks more gibberish as he picks up my wrist to check my pulse. It's strange because I'm seeing all of this happen, but I can't speak, move, or hear anything. It's like a dream. And just as I realize this, my eyes close.

My ears ring, and the only feeling I can comprehend is vastness.

CHAPTER 7

I can hear again. A voice speaks. No, not one. Multiple voices. They don't sound as garbled, but it's hard to understand them with this massive headache. I keep my eyes closed to wait and see if the pain will fade. Three recognizable voices argue, though I can't yet tell whose voice is who, and my sense of smell starts to come back to me. Old paper. The precinct.

"—Fysher, get ahold of yourself. There's nothing we can do at the moment."

"I told you it was too early to send her on a mission, Bennet! I'm not the one responsible for a drugged agent."

"Oh, she'll wake up soon, anyway."

"She knew the risks. Luis, Mr. Bennet, you should know better than to bicker over something so senseless."

"Our mission was almost compromised because we put too much trust in Charlotte. I'm not the commander of this mission, so whose fault is it, really?"

"Are we really placing blame now? Because I have a few ideas—"

"Shush, she's moving!"

My eyes open, and I'm relieved to be in a dimly lit room, not the bar with its strobe lights. All eyes focus on me. I find myself lounging in a chair in the corner. I look around, my head pulsing, and notice red marks around my wrists, like rope was tied around them.

"What happened?" I say, my voice almost a whisper. I feel sick, like the energy I had earlier has been ripped away. *How long has it been?*

Bree seems to read my mind. "You've been passed out for close to half an hour. Not too long," she says carefully, watching me. They're all watching me. Why? For amusement?

She speaks again. "It seems that in the time you looked away from your drink, our suspect switched the glasses. We didn't want to tell you before, but his background check pins him as a medically diagnosed psychopath. He's charming, kind, and very manipulative. He had you from the start, Charlie. After you fell unconscious, he tied your hands to keep you from moving, then directed the car to travel to some unknown location. Luckily, Luis was able to hack the car, and we brought it back here."

I stared at them in disbelief. *This* is the danger I've put myself in? Is this my fault? No. It's not. They made the mistake of sending me in without any training or instruction. It doesn't matter that they saved me. What could have happened if they weren't able to direct the car back to the precinct? Would I have been kept in some dark room, held for days on end? I could have been seriously hurt, or worse. I gulp, not wanting to think about the latter.

"I know what you're thinking," Luis says, leaning on his arm against the computer desk. "We didn't train you. And you're right. It wasn't exactly our top priority. We thought you might know some of the basics. Your school curriculum requires self-defense classes."

"Well aren't you a bunch of Einsteins. I'm in advanced courses for my age. I took self-defense years ago. I'm rusty."

"Charlie, please understand. The government didn't give us many regulations for running EASY. This is all a test run. We'll make a few mistakes. We understand if you want to quit."

I could give up, of course, save everyone the trouble, but I've never been one to pass on an opportunity. I don't just back down.

I gain my composure, sitting up straighter. "Before we take any further steps, I'd like training. *Real* training. Puzzles, coding, self-defense. The whole shebang."

Out of the corner of my eye, I see Orson's eyebrows rise. I can sense that he's shocked. They're all shocked. Any sensible person would have quit. But I'm not one of those people. Luis nods. Good. I'll start training. I stand, feeling a little wobbly, but refuse to show it. *Where am I?*

The room has one door and one completely dark glass pane, nothing like the crystal-clear windows of the school. A desktop computer sits on a table in front of the window, the kind of desktop that is only used by the few people who work in offices, and there are a few chairs lined on the back wall facing the glass pane. I assume it's to observe, but observe what, exactly?

Luis leans comfortably in his chair and examines his fingernails, then glances up at me. His piercing blue eyes watch mine as he stands. He tilts his head at Bree, and she immediately understands. She sits in front of the desktop and starts to type. I glance at Orson, who is eating a sandwich. Luis looks back to me, his attention now undivided, and slides into the chair next to mine.

"This is the observation side of the interrogation room. Our suspect, Joseph Foster, is on the other side. Don't worry, you won't have to talk to him. That's what EASY is for. It's stress-free for everyone, a win-win. Hopefully, with your new training—which will go along with your regular missions—capturing suspects will be stress-free for you, too. Bree, I feel that we've left Mr. Foster waiting long enough. Let's begin the interrogation."

I perk up, my curiosity spiked. Luis presses the screen on the wall, and the blackness of the glass pane is replaced with the image of Joseph Foster with his torso and feet secured to a chair, in the middle of a stark-white room. He looks forward, almost staring into Luis' eyes, though I know he can't see us on the other side of the glass. Orson steps into the room with a vial of liquid and hands it to Joseph, who stares back expressionless. Orson waits while he downs the drink. He's so calm. What a maniac. I should have guessed that he was a psychopath.

Orson walks back into our side of the room and resumes eating his sandwich. I ignore him, investing my attention into what's about to happen. Without warning, Joseph's head drops and he's unconscious. A few moments later, an almost movie-like image flickers to life on the desktop. I can see the world from Joseph's perspective, just as I had imagined before. How he sees people, what he pays attention to. I sit next to Bree and Luis, observing the screen. Joseph seems to be in an apartment, speaking to a strange woman with heavy blush and dark eyeshadow.

"I hope you're aware that I'm not doing this for free," the Joseph on the screen says in an icy voice.

"Of course not. I would have never expected that from someone who does what you do. What do you charge?" the unrecognizable face replies.

"For three? Thirty thousand."

"You people aren't cheap. Just do the job."

"I never miss."

"It's a group. They should be at the music store tomorrow at 8:00. You have the file. Don't miss it."

"I won't."

The scene continues with the exchange of money, and I'm captivated by it all. Luis glances at Bree, and she responds by fast-forwarding the memory to a day after the deal. The eyes of the screen now show a bird's-eye view of a crowd surrounding a music store. A banner above the shop reads "Opening, with brand-new guitars: play from your mind!" A terrible idea, I admit, but this crowd seems to be clawing at the door. Who is Joseph aiming for?

It takes a minute or two for Joseph to flip open his silver rifle case and assemble the weapon, attaching a suppressor to the end of the barrel to decrease the chances of detection. He glances around at the rooftop he's on and adjusts his bi-pod to better hold his weapon.

Joseph squints down at the crowd and then through the scope of his gun, going back and forth between the magnified view and his own to find his targets.

He tilts his face down and peers through the scope of his weapon, zooming in toward a group of six businessmen within the crowd, all conversing with one another. They all have an aura of confidence. Joseph zooms in even closer, focusing on the tallest. He aims. In the blink of an eye, the tallest man's head snaps back. He falls over, and a dark liquid stains the ground.

Joseph has shot the tallest of the six men.

I stare as screams erupt from the crowd. They run. The businessmen split up while one stays by the side of the bleeding man, trying to get him to move. Joseph wastes no time, and the one beside the bleeding body falls over, landing on top of the first man. More dark liquid oozes onto the cement.

The view through the scope zooms out, searching for a third victim. Joseph finds his target among the panicked crowd and pulls the trigger. The third body falls among the running men, women, and children. Sirens blast from a distance. We see through Joseph's eyes as he packs his things calmly. The screen darkens as he slips sunglasses on. Luis shuts the video off.

"And there's our proof," Luis says, leaning back, unfazed by the grim scene we witnessed. I scan the room, and the others' expressions match his. I feel drowned, having just watched a massacre. I put a hand over my mouth. What did those men do to deserve such a brutal and public death? Joseph didn't care. He just put bullets through three people and left. Would I have met the same fate if my mission had not been pulled back onto the right track?

"A triple murder," I mumble as Joseph starts to wake up. I clench my fist, feeling it shake with anger. I want to scream at him, try to make his ill mind understand the lives he ended.

But he couldn't understand. A psychopath can't empathize. It is such a terrible feeling when you can't get through to a person. When their mind can't comprehend the point you're making. Does he even realize what he did wrong? Regardless of what those men may have done, they had lives. Maybe even families. Now they have nothing.

Bree nods at my comment, standing. "Let's charge him and go. It's been a long workday," she says.

"Ditto." Orson stands, having finished his sandwich.

I glare at them. "Are you two serious? What is wrong with you people?"

"Charlie, we can't waste time grieving over people who are gone," Luis says. "Let's focus on the present. We've got the killer. Justice is being served."

I decide not to respond, watching as Joseph snaps out of his daze. He clutches his head and doubles over, shuddering. Two uniformed women enter the room, unlock him, and take him out. He will probably get a sentence of life in prison. There's nothing I can do now.

Bree and Orson gather their files and paperwork and exit. I look out of the door and see Orson close his office door behind him and Bree slip into the conference room.

"He . . . Joseph Foster was in *pain*," I say.

Luis looks up. "That's expected. We're still in the program's trial, after all. Subjects will experience physical pain and possible lasting trauma as a result of interfering with the limbic system."

"Huh?"

"The EASY program works best when users experience the pain and emotion of their memories to their full extent. We tap into the limbic system within the brain to unlock those feelings. The effects fade within a few hours to a week," he mumbles the last few words.

"That's terrible."

"It's just a kink in the programming," he says, then brings his happy tone back to say, "We'll fix it over time, so don't let it bog you down. Go home, Charlotte. It's been a long day. You've done good work here, and your training starts tomorrow." Luis smiles, patting me on the shoulder. He shuts the equipment down and walks out.

Thoughts swim in my mind. *So, we're supposed to infiltrate the minds of others and go home without a second thought?*

I look around the room, thinking of all of the fights I could have with him, with Bree, with Orson. But my workday is over and there's no use. They wouldn't listen to my reasoning. I walk out of the room, into the lobby, and I am stopped by Honey Adler. She offers me a ride home. Though taking a ride in Honey's car is the last thing I need, it's getting dark out, and after the afternoon I had, I couldn't handle the walk home.

I get in her car and stare out of the window. We pull out of the precinct.

A siren blares, the sound originating from a police car. I see Joseph in the back. Joseph watches me as they pass, and I shiver, recalling the crime he committed.

Am I any better than him? I've committed a crime. Not a massacre, but still, a crime. I face my act by doing my time every day at the precinct, but is it good enough? Am I good enough?

CHAPTER 8

"Is there something you're not telling me?"

Mom has asked this every day since I joined EASY. She tosses me one of those mom-looks that seems to whisper *I can see right through your lies.* As much as I want to tell her about my new work, I couldn't possibly let her worry about my safety at the precinct.

I shovel some mashed sweet potatoes into my mouth. "No. Come on, mom, you know I tell you everything."

"Everything, huh?"

We stare at one another for who knows how long. I can feel my poker face start to falter as mom's competitive spirit glints in her eyes. I can tell the chicken curry on my plate is getting cold, so in the interest of ending this showdown—and in the interest of keeping my dignity by straying from a fight I know I'll lose—I stuff as much food into my mouth as will fit and rise from my chair.

Mom sighs and throws her arms in the air. "Well, Charlie, I guess you've won this one."

"I guess I have," I say, though my voice is muffled. I have to spit half of my lunch into the trash to prevent myself from choking to death. "I'll catch ya on the flip side, relic."

"Relic?" she gasps, like I've injured her soul, and places a hand over her heart. "Excuse you, missy, but *I* am no relic."

I know I haven't actually hurt her. She and I did this when I was younger. Overreact to everything and the reality doesn't seem so bad in retrospect. But as life got harder in the past year, our little joke faded away.

I return her tone. "Yes, yes, I *know*. You're Mrs. 'Best Generation.' Whatever, relic, you're old news! Go back to your dangly bracelets and hooded sweatshirts and leave us advanced teens alone."

This makes mom laugh, and I laugh with her.

"Charlie, if you knew half of what we went through . . . well, never mind."

Immediately, I'm thrown back into that book and Luis' lecture. I can hear his voice: "I want you to *understand*. I want you to be *passionate*."

Wow. I'm a jerk.

I really don't know half of what she went through. My mom is full of stories, and I've never cared to ask for one. My expression darkens and I sit back at the table.

"No, mom. Tell me."

She is still chuckling from the earlier insult. "What's that?"

"What was it like for you? Before I was born?"

"Oh," she says after a moment. "That's a lot to ask for, Charlie."

"Then pick something and tell me about it. I'm reading this book called *The '20s: A Government Restructured.* But you're right here! Living history. What was a car wash like? Were you scared of the dangers of public schools? Did kids smoke all the time, and were you in all of those protests? Did you know anyone in those riots?"

"Whoa, Charlie, slow down. We have a lifetime to talk about this, but it's refreshing that you're asking." She searches my eyes. "*Is there* anything you're not telling me? If anything is happening—"

"I'm fine, mom."

"Okay. You know I worry. There are some people out there—" I know what she's about to say, and I've heard this warning a million times.

"Mom, I'm genuinely curious. Please?"

"Let's take five and meet up when I think of a story."

After five minutes, I am holding a steaming mug of instant hot cocoa and my mom plops two mint marshmallows in.

"Let's see . . . did you know school used to be eight hours a day and would start at seven-thirty or eight a.m.? Or . . . did you know that cellular devices were rectangles that could hold dozens of games?" She looks at me, and my face is slack, so she continues. "Let me think of something interesting . . . have you ever heard of fidget spinners?"

"Mom, I want to know about *you.*"

She sits across from me and slides her own mug of hot cocoa closer. "I used to live in a place called Seattle. You may know it as a larger area named Princeton Village."

"That's where most of the boarding schools are."

"Yes, they built many, many higher-level schools for children around the time you were born. Anyway, I grew up in the suburbs.

You know: two brothers, a dalmatian, your grandparents, and a fridge full of soda. I won't bore you with the details, Charlie, but Grandma Brandy, Grandpa Elan, and Uncle Finn didn't survive the Great Pandemic. Your other uncle moved to Australia to help the vaccine effort. I haven't heard from him since."

"And the dalmatian?"

A smile plays on my mom's lips. I'm not sure if the joke was appropriate, but I was expecting a happier story.

"The dog, Archer, found a happy home with a neighbor." She stops for a quick hot cocoa break. "I changed everything about myself. My freshman year of high school—uh, that would be your fifth or sixth level of school—I got 50s in my work. I was glued to my phone, and I skipped class whenever I could. I stayed that way until the pandemic. It took four funerals for me to turn my life around. That's when the protests kicked off.

"My second year of college, I met your father. He was a business major. We decided to transfer to another school, and we soon found an apartment, far away from Seattle. It's a good thing we moved to a smaller town, too. The more populated cities were infected the fastest, then turned into mass education districts and hospital centers, or just continued on with a much smaller population."

She continues talking about her life. Sure, I did *ask* her to tell me about the '20s, but I'm exhausted from the Joseph situation last night and she can probably tell I'm starting to nod off.

A few minutes later, my eyes float open, and I notice we're on the couch. Mom has an arm wrapped around me as she flicks through digital work files. She glances down at me.

"Charlie, I'm not sure how much you heard earlier, but I want your teen years to be better than mine. You deserve to be a normal teenager. I don't know why you're coming home late and leaving so early, aside from your assigned work at the precinct, and I won't inquire any further if you don't want me to. Just . . . promise that whatever you do, you'll be safe. Okay?"

I don't think I'm fully awake, but I do know that I'd never want to disappoint her. I respond with a firm nod.

"Goodnight, Charlie."

I give her an awkward half-smile and let my eyelids weigh themselves down. I drift off again. *Good night, mom.*

CHAPTER 9

Day one. The start of my training. Luis has instructed me to meet him at a karate studio downtown, alone. He also told me to wear something to work out in, so I dressed in a simple black tank top and purple sweatpants. Not the most fashion-forward choice, I'll admit, but I'm not here to walk down the red carpet. I'm here to learn skills I will need to follow the path I've chosen.

I walk to the karate studio and crash straight into the door. I let out a surprised noise, something like "GERBALERF" that definitely wasn't English, realizing this door doesn't slide on its own. I rub my cheek with my knuckles. This studio must be older than me. Its doors have handles. I grab the handle, letting the door to the boarded-up building creak open, and make my way inside.

The inside is somehow even more ancient than the outside. Sure, it doesn't have vines growing on the walls or windows that are cracked, but it's a giant room with scattered exercise equipment and target boards along the walls. There is a large space with a concrete floor in the middle, which, I assume, is used for sparring. Any window has been covered with wooden planks, but small rays of light shine between the boards. It's strange, but there is no glass in the frames, which allows small drops of rain to seep through the wooden planks. I can see the second level of the building through gaps where ceiling panels have fallen from the upper floor.

I look around. No sign of Luis. I should at least warm up. I flip a small white switch on the wall. After a moment, fluorescent lights flicker on, one by one. I'm surprised the electricity still works. Clenching my jaw, I take a swing at a punching bag. Just before my fist makes contact, something warm grasps my wrist. Out of reflex, I spin, and my other fist swings, but the hand stops me again.

I look up. It's Luis, and he's *fast*. Faster than I thought. We watch each other for a moment. What does he expect me to do? I wait for him to say something, but no words come from him, and his eyes are locked on me.

"If you continue to punch with a full fist, you'll deform your hand," he says finally.

With the hand that isn't holding my fist, he punches me in the stomach, knocking the wind out of me. Unfortunately, I can't see whether he uses his full fist or not. I stumble back. Luis, without blinking an eye, crouches and sweeps my feet off the floor with his leg. I collapse onto the concrete ground, gasping for air. I hear the thudding of feet and look up to realize that I'm now alone. He must have run off.

I stand, finding my shirt covered in dust and dirt. *Is he testing me?* I guess the purpose of this exercise is to find Luis and defeat him, but

I'm disappointed that there were no instructions. Maybe that's the point, to expect the unexpected. Brushing the dust off, I look around, searching for clues as to where Luis went. *Come on, Charlie. Expect the unexpected.* I force my eyes to look for anything out of the ordinary and find myself pinpointing a door in the corner of the room, cracked open.

I discover a carpeted staircase, nearly coated in dried mud. It seems that no one has been in this building to vacuum. Luckily, the lack of cleaning allows me to see the new footprints. *Luis.* I slowly make my way up the stairs, step by step. My breathing is shallow, and my heart rate is rapid, but I somehow manage to remain silent and, hopefully, undetected.

I make my way to the upper level. It used to be an office, with empty desks and filing cabinets still in place. Wow, this building must be older than I thought. It's been quite a while since anyone has occupied this large of a workspace for a desk job.

One of the remnants of previous generations—a time when most worked in offices and suffocating cubicles, gossiping by the water cooler. At least, that's what relic television shows tell me.

Multiple doors open into this level, making it the perfect hiding place. My first step makes the floor creak. There are several large holes in the floor, as I had observed earlier from the ground floor. Treading a dangerous jungle, alert and vigilant, I tiptoe through the office.

I hop over a small hole. Luis doesn't seem to be here. Maybe I went the wrong way. Or maybe this isn't a test. But why would Luis be doing this if it wasn't a test? He's trying to see whether I can easily find criminals, to do my job correctly. If I had been given this training before I was sent into the field, I could have dealt with Joseph. I wouldn't have looked like an idiot on my first mission. *They* made me look stupid.

I hear a creak behind me, and whip around to face my opponent, but I'm too late. Luis has grabbed my arm and flung me to the ground. I wince, rubbing my arm. I narrow my eyes. *He's going to be sorry in a minute.* But I can't bring myself to fight back. This won't end well.

"What's the matter, Charlotte? Scared?" Luis smirks. I've never seen this side of him before. He went from Smart-Goody-Two-Shoes to Self-Defense-Expert. And I thought *I* was the one pretending. God, everyone could be fake.

There's no way I'm going to let him push me around like this, especially if it's all a test. I can't look like an idiot to Orson, Bree, or Luis. The man in front of me watches, judging. His hair, weighed down by sweat, falls into his face. Disgusting. He's expecting me to do something.

"I'm not scared. Just waiting," I reply.

"For what?"

"You'll see."

"I'm ready for whatever it is, Charlie."

I'm not sure what I'm waiting for. I just need to stall until I can think of a better plan. Or any plan at all. I need an impulse decision, and I need it now. I need that *Charlie attitude* to help me. It certainly didn't help at the Busy Tuxedo the other day. I wait a few more moments, letting Luis catch his breath, and do the first thing I can think of. There's an open space in the floor directly behind Luis, and I bring my foot up from the wooden floor to kick him into it. Not the smartest decision, I'll admit, but effective.

Luis gives me a startled look, falling back into the space in the floor and disappearing. He tries to catch himself on the edge, but his hand slips. I hear a yell, then . . . Silence. There's no way he survived that fall. Am I now *Charlie Starborne: . . . Murderer?* Will I have to change my name and move to New Zealand? Was Orson right? Am I truly a criminal? *I'm a murderer.*

I rush to the gap. Luis lies on a large air mattress, looking up at me. He smiles, and I let a deep breath out. He's okay. Did he know I was going to push him through the hole in the floor? The taste of blood teases my mouth, and I run down the stairs to the air mattress. This is crazy. Maybe I'm dreaming. I killed Luis, and now I'm in shock.

I carefully approach the deathbed, and as sure as I breathe, Luis is there. He sits up calmly, checking his watch. Our eyes meet. He stands, brushing himself off. We remain silent, and my face must be white as a sheet, but my anger quickly boils. I hope my face is flushing crimson, so Luis understands the emotional rollercoaster he sent me on.

"What . . . how . . . that's not possible!" I say, straining to say the correct words. But Luis' reaction is the opposite of what I thought it would be. He simply chuckles, and I'm ready to explode. Luis puts a hand on my arm, and I move it away.

"Don't touch me."

"Charlie, I can tell you're mad—"

"Try furious."

"It was a test—"

"I'm aware." I refuse to give him the satisfaction of finishing his sentences.

"You passed, Charlie."

I look up at him, lacking the words to express my anger. Not that he would care anyway. Espresso-colored locks of hair blow into my face, partially blocking my vision, and I quickly brush them behind my ear. Wind whistles between the wooden planks over the windowpanes. The weather has changed. *How long have I been here?*

I push my anger to the back of my mind for a time when I might need it, and see Luis' jacket, neatly folded on a sidewall. I grab it, turning to leave. My shoulder slams into Luis' arm as I walk to the door, and I can feel his eyes watching me. I watch my fingertips turn white from pressure as they struggle to push the door open. The wooden exit gives way, allowing me to pass. I limp out, my body aching.

If I can't last in a fight against a nerd like Luis, how will I ever be able to go up against the jerks and manipulative criminals I'm likely to face? I am weak. I hear a *ding*, which means I've received a message, and check my watch. It's Luis.

Great match today. See you tomorrow. Same place.

I pull Luis' jacket around my torso, the breeze lightly tossing branches back and forth. I guess I'll have to do the same thing tomorrow.

Oh my God.

CHAPTER 10

My eyes pull themselves open. The room is dark. It must still be night.
My bedroom looks different. The drawer where my shirts were placed
is now gone, and the nightstand where my page-reader is set has moved
to the corner. Strange, I didn't move anything. As I scan the room, I
notice a tall, dark, and husky silhouette in the corner, observing me
with illuminated white eyes. It doesn't scare me, though my heart
should be in my throat right now. We watch each other for a moment,
the figure standing there, unblinking.

What do you want from me? I ask.

The thing you love the most, the demon says in a misty voice.

What is this, some type of sleep paralysis? That's it. I'm asleep. All
I have to do is pinch myself. But I can't seem to get my arms to move.
There must be another way to get this vision out of my room.

I can hear your loud thoughts. You can't get rid of me, the demon
says. *I'll be here until I get what I want. Your joy.*

I don't know what you're talking about, I respond.

You'll find out soon enough. The vision grins from ear to ear, then vanishes.

My bedroom morphs into Mr. Ariosto's classroom, and it's midday. I can hear my classmates behind me without turning around, or perhaps I can't force myself to move from my spot. Mr. Ariosto is saying words, though I can't hear what they are. He asks a question of a boy I recognize. The boy's cheek bears a bruise, his lip is split, and his right eye is swollen shut. His name is at the tip of my tongue, but I can't place it. The boy smirks at me, and though his words are unintelligible, the tone of his voice is smooth and light.

Mr. Ariosto turns to me as if expecting an answer to a question I was never given. I just smile in reply, and he repeats his words, this time audible.

"'Life must be understood backward, but it must be lived forward.' Do you know who that is from, Ms. Starborne?"

"I don't believe so."

I must have been given this quote somewhere before, I just can't think of it right now. Why was it important, anyway? I'm the only one with actual potential in the class. He should be picking on the kids telling meaningless jokes in the back. He asks me again.

"Ms. Starborne, who gave us that quote?"

I say only what I can think of. "I don't know."

"The answer is Kierkegaard. Pay attention next time."

I want to fight back, but the classroom morphs into a dock. I am at the edge, looking out at an endless body of water and a foggy horizon. I look around and there is no visible land. Just me, a dock, and the ocean surrounding us. I take a moment to stare down into the water, furrowing my brow. As I lean further, I get a clearer view of myself. Or rather, a perfect version of myself. No cuts, no bruises, no rings of purple under my eyes. Just me, smiling back.

Something kicks me into the water. I turn my body as I descend to see Luis, Orson, and Bree standing tall on the dock, watching me drown. They do nothing, their eyes blank. In the water, I take a few breaths. These breaths are different from the ones I take in the air. Deeper. More peaceful.

There is nothing underwater. No fish, no plants . . . absolutely nothing. All I can see are a few lonely feet ahead of me. I make my way through the water, not struggling against a current. An instinct, some might say, but it is more like a magnetic tug.

I get to my unknown destination, and my mother is there, floating upright. She smiles, her eyes as dead as Luis, Bree, and Orson's were. Almost like the demon before. But she is different. My mother is not my enemy, she's my best friend.

What's going on? I say.

Oh, Charlie, don't you know? Your life is about to go in a new and exciting direction. Be ready for an adventure, my Charlotte, she replies, happy as ever, her worries washed away by the endless sea.

Mom, what are you talking about? I don't want things to change. I love my life right now. My ignorance glows in my argumentation.

I love you is all she says before I snap awake.

CHAPTER 11

My brain tries to pound out of my skull, like a prisoner in a cell, as I open my eyes. Good. It's actually morning this time. The aches of the past month come back to me one by one. It's been the same routine every day. School, sparring with Luis at the karate studio, learning coding and programming back at the precinct with Bree, then homework from Orson. All topped off with a few missions here and there. This time, though, they've made sure not to throw me into the field without information. I've been getting home at about 11:15 p.m. every day, and it seems to take a toll on my mental health. *Organize, practice, study,* my associates drill into my head.

I carefully sit up. Three and a half weeks with no mercy shown from the rest of the team. Nothing some Agalferal won't fix. I grab the pain medication off my nightstand and examine the label. I had my mom order a few bottles after the third day of torturous training. I swallow a pill with a large gulp of water, willing myself to stand.

I hobble through my room, feeling any sudden movement might

cause me to snap in half. I grab a dark green bag from atop my dresser, piling book upon book inside. Orson really has no mercy when it comes to studying. He's not the best in the motivation department either, but I'll keep that to myself.

Three more cases have rolled into the precinct during my training. Our latest, Elenora Patel, blackmailed her cousin for tens of thousands of dollars and killed him when he couldn't pay any more. That case took two days, during which Orson and I partnered up to catch her. Luis thought it would be better to have help on missions. *Training wheels*, he'd called it.

We went on a stakeout, and I found Orson wasn't as terrible as I'd first perceived him to be. He has a sister. Well, had. He disowned her after she was given a sentence of fifteen years without parole. He wouldn't tell me why, but he didn't need to.

We talked about school, work, and movies. Turns out we have more in common than I thought. When we finally booked Elenora Patel, we agreed that he was still the grumpy boss, and I was still the stubborn delinquent. Orson and I decided not to speak of the stakeout after that. But in the back of my mind, I think I see him as a sort of father figure, and I think he sees me as more than a delinquent, too.

As I slip on my shoes, memories of last night flash in my head, chilling the room.

I'll be here until I get what I want. Your joy.

Life must be understood backward, but it must be lived forward.

Your life is about to go in a new and exciting direction. Be ready for an adventure.

Then I remember a face from the dream. A face of a boy from a terrible memory. I can place the name now, though I'm scared to even think it.

I tremble, nearly falling out of my socks, but quickly shake the feeling. It was just a dream—if you could even call it that. More like a tranquil nightmare. I put the bag over my shoulder. A sting shoots up my arm, but the Agalferal quickly overtakes it. The sweet absence of pain. I welcome the numbness as I walk downstairs.

My mom is at the table eating. Having learned from the past few weeks that I don't have enough time for a sit-down breakfast, she hands me a bagel and a banana and throws a quick "love you" my way. I step out the door, the fresh breeze filling my lungs. This is it. My big day. Tomorrow, I become a free woman, no longer forced to work for the precinct, but working there by choice.

This must be the change mentioned in my dream. I'm getting over my past mistakes and living my life the way I want to live it. They'll unlock the shackles and let me roam. Dream Mom was right: my life is about to take a new and exciting path. If I survive my final mission as a criminal this evening, I can come back tomorrow and be sent on missions as a normal citizen. It's almost too good to be true, but I've served my time. I deserve it.

School flashes by in an instant. Before I know it, the clock on the wall reads 12:30 in the afternoon, and my feet are carrying me to the precinct. The doors slide open, my nose recognizing the familiar scent of pencil shavings. It's a big mission tonight, and we're having a small celebration of my freedom afterward, so Orson insisted I skip training today. Not that there's much left to learn anyway. I learn faster than any mentor can teach.

I'm instantly greeted by Honey Adler, her yellow, sparkly blouse blinding me. Her nose crinkles, highlighting her usual happy attitude. I sign in for the last time, walking to the conference room. Orson and Bree are already waiting for me.

"There she is!" Bree says, gleaming. "How does it feel knowing you're almost done with your sentence?"

"Relieving," I respond, feeling more comfortable in this office than I did several weeks ago. I sit in my usual chair, spinning lightly. "Where's Luis?"

"He should be here soon," Orson grumbles. "Had some matters to attend to."

"Forgot to have your morning coffee, Orson?" I smirk.

"I'm going to the Blue Office," he says.

The Blue Office. Orson's sanctuary. I've never seen anyone but him or Honey go inside.

"No time for that," Bree pushes her glasses up, folding her hands on the table. "We're all just a little exhausted. Today's case is a big one, Charlie," she says. "We're trying to catch a well-known multi-billionaire who, we have been informed, could be the mastermind behind a massive drug trafficking business. He has a company, of course, but we believe that's just a front."

Orson nods, leaning against the wall. "The three of us have been up all night, setting up the EASY program and finding everything we can about our suspect. Hell, we know what he dressed up as for Halloween thirty years ago. Luis has been doing most of the work. He just left to acquire a few documents from city hall."

I sit up. "So, what business does this multi-billionaire run?" I say, interested.

"I'm sure you've heard of EarthKey?" Bree tilts her head.

"The . . . tech company? The one you based the EASY program off?" I slowly reach into my pocket, getting a small white container out of it. I read "EarthKey" from the label. These tiny orange pills are distributed by a drug lord? I set the box onto the table, feeling disconnected from what was once an escape.

I'm too invested in inspecting the capsule that I don't notice Luis trudging in with an armful of folders and documents. I look up, seeing his sunken eyes and uncombed hair. I guess I've been so busy focusing on my training that I hardly realized how hard Orson, Bree, and Luis have been working.

Orson's jacket is wrinkled. In any other case, he would have made sure to get it cleaned and pressed as soon as possible. I've also noticed that his attitude has been worse lately and he has been more irritable over little things. Bree doesn't look any better. She tries to hide her fatigue more than the men, keeping her hair neatly brushed and her posture upright. But I've noticed delayed responses to my endless questions, and Bree cannot camouflage her lack of energy. These three have been working much harder than me. They must be really invested in this project.

"Did you tell her everything?" Luis says, yawning.

"I am about to. Feed the documents into the computer while Orson and I explain tonight's mission," Bree responds as she stands, turning the digital cube on to project an outline of everything I need to know. Luis makes his exit, groggy from sleep deprivation.

Bree pushes her glasses up. "The man's name is Dexter Thomas. You must sneak into his office, which is on the 34th floor of his company's building, and hack into the documents on his desktop. These documents should be in code. Don't worry, we'll pick up everything you're hearing and seeing from your ear- and eyepieces."

"So, what's so different about this mission?"

"Well," Orson drawls as he leans against the wall. "We still need Dexter's confession. Hopefully, by the time you're done looking over the documents, he'll be coming back from a meeting."

"You're purposefully putting me in danger? I don't have an escape, Orson! It's thirty-four flights up."

"Relax, Starborne. We know that he has no experience in self-defense. He depends on his security team to protect him. From the precinct, Bree will shut down the earpieces that connect Dexter to his entire security team and put old footage into the eyes of the cameras. They won't have any idea what's going on."

"Well, how am I supposed to get out of there with an unconscious forty-something-year-old man?"

Luis' voice adds from the other room, "I'll be flying a techno-copter outside of the window."

Orson narrows his eyes, clearing his throat. "While that is true, the techno-copter can only fit two. Luis and the suspect. You'll have to find your own way out."

I nod. "When are we starting the mission?"

Bree and Orson glance at each other. Bree smiles. "Fifteen minutes. Go change into the clothes that are laid out for you in the bathroom. Meet us back here in three."

"Go," Orson says.

I stand, walking out. My brain is going in two different directions.

One on the approaching mission, and the other on that haunting nightmare. I shake the latter from my mind, focusing on what's important—getting out of this assignment alive so I can achieve the freedom I've earned. But what will happen when I'm free? Will I continue down this path? Can I trust myself to make the right decisions again?

Who will I be?

CHAPTER 12

I mess with the string of pearls around my neck, watching the trees pass by from the safety of the limo. The GPS blinks, telling me that we're almost at the EarthKey office. I take a deep breath and fix my suit jacket. There's only so much primping I can do before I arrive. The limo slows to a stop and the doors hiss open.

Just act confident, I tell myself. I make a beeline to the front desk. A woman looks up, and I present a pass, showing her that I'm Mr. Thomas's personal assistant. Orson designed it to be foolproof, like the card at the bar. She glides a scanner over the pass, and the light buzzes green. The woman smiles, motioning for me to enter the door to her left.

Staying silent, I make my way to the staircase. I'm less likely to be spotted here. On the elevator, I might come face-to-face with someone who, unlike the secretary I'd just met, knows Dexter Thomas's actual personal assistant. I count each flight as I advance to the 34th floor.

12 . . . 18 . . . 26 . . . I'm starting to lose track. And my breath.

"Almost there, Charlie," a voice chirps in my ear. It's Bree.

I stop climbing, looking up at the flights to come. I don't think I'll have enough energy by the time I get to the office.

"You've got to go. You're wasting time," Orson says. I roll my eyes, starting to jog to the top.

27 . . . 29 . . . 34. Finally.

I take a moment for a breath until I hear Orson's frustrated "Go!" from the device in my ear. I walk down the well-lit hallway, passing pictures of a man shaking hands with the mayor, the governor, and with the CEO of Wrennprice, another tech company. I recognize his pristine haircut and arched nose from the files: it's Dexter.

A man sits at a desk beside a closed door, talking to, what seems to be, no one. He must have an earpiece, too.

"Sir, Mr. Thomas has a meeting right now. He can speak to you later. No, I cannot assure you what time he can call back. Mr. Thomas is a very busy man. Can I put you on hold, Mr. Rabinowitz?" He taps the digital cube lying on his desk and picks up another call. "Yes, Penelope? Yes, the drink on his desk has been refilled. Lemonade, as requested this morning."

The man glances at me. "Penelope, I have to go." He taps the cube again and turns his full attention to me. "How can I help you?"

"I have an appointment with Dexter."

"Dexter?" I assume most don't call him by his first name. This secretary can guess I know him personally.

The man nods, scrolling through his desktop screen with his finger.

"I don't see an appointment here."

"Really?" I say.

"Are you with another company? Perhaps an intern?"

"You must have me mistaken, sir." I walk over to the desk and flip the screen around to face me.

I can almost hear Bree and Orson's disapproval from the precinct. "Careful, Charlotte. You're in dangerous waters. This is an international company. Not a school principal's office," Orson warns.

I smirk, glancing at the man. He quickly flips the screen back around. "Ma'am, I can't authorize that."

"Charlotte," Orson hisses. "We're working on the appointment. Be patient."

"Ma'am." The secretary watches me carefully. I expect Orson knows exactly what I'm thinking. Adrenaline rushes to my head as I take a small green capsule out of my pocket. The secretary reaches for his digital cube, most likely to call for help. I fling myself over the desk and grab the man's arm, forcing the tablet through his closed teeth. He struggles as I cover his mouth until I'm sure he's passed out. The capsule did exactly what Bree said it would. *Thank you, Bree.*

"Charlotte!" Orson roars. "That was not the agreed-upon plan!"

I chuckle, pressing a button under the desk. I hear a click, and the door slides open. "Oh, Orson, who cares about plans? That's so 2030. This is so much more fun."

Bree whispers from the other side of the line, trying to calm Orson down. I ignore them, entering the room. The office is big. There are couches in the center of the room. Trophies, degrees, and plaques line the back wall, on shelves and in picture frames. On the other wall is a portrait of my opponent, who will soon arrive. Below it is a desk. I sink into the desk chair. I can tell it's expensive and I spin around in it. The chair makes me feel like I'm sitting on a cloud. I could stay here forever—

"You have a job to do," Bree says, interrupting my thoughts. I sit up, take another green capsule out of my pocket, and toss it into the fresh jug of lemonade next to me. It'll take a minute or two to dissolve.

"How much time do I have?" I tap the center of the desk, and a hologram appears in front of me. I look through the drawers, toss aside a phone or two, and find the computer's wireless controller: a black glove.

"About nine minutes."

"Only nine?"

"We have the entry code, and hacking the files shouldn't take long. I'll guide you."

I put the glove on, hold my hand in the air, and face the screen. After Luis gives me the password, I start scrolling through the contents of the computer. Bree taught me to expect a more advanced screen mode, and the computer's sensor picks up the motion of my hand. Photo Gallery, Phone, Drawing Board, Printer . . . *Where are the documents?* I scroll once more and an error message pops up on the display, followed by a screen of white numbers and letters.

"Bree?"

"Got it."

Bree starts giving me directions and I catch on quickly, typing in mid-air. Sweat trickles down the side of my face. Blinking it out of my eyes, I continue to type nonsensical numbers into the computer. I click Enter and the digits stop dancing for a moment. The screen goes blank. I wait for something to happen. I don't know what I'm waiting for exactly, but I use this time to get some updates.

"What's the update on the secretary? When I left him, he was out like a light."

"He's awake," Bree says. "Thinks he just fell asleep on the job. He doesn't remember a thing."

"Good."

Orson growls, "You got lucky this time, Starborne."

The screen blinks back on and a new background appears. This one is filled with files. I start scrolling through them, clicking on a random pick. It shows me pages and pages of some legal document that I don't care about. Useless.

"I don't understand, Bree. Where are the documents on drug exchanges?"

Bree's usual innocent voice doesn't respond.

"Bree? Bree, hello? Orson, are you there?" I continue to scroll through the files with no luck. I jump when a small hologram pops up beside the desktop. It shows a man—the man in the portrait behind me—speaking to the secretary. This must be his security system. Dexter is back from his meeting, and I'm here looking through his private computer.

I turn off the display and look around, my heart pounding. I rush to the only other door in the room. I'm out of breath, and my thoughts are quick and simple. The door slides open. I go inside. It hisses closed behind me and a light flickers on above me. I'm in a closet. Coats, suits, and ties line the walls of the miniature boutique. I start walking around as I hear the main entrance to the office open. Footsteps follow.

Remaining quiet, I start exploring the area. It's my best bet, for now. Bree and Orson have ghosted on me, and I'll have plenty of time in here until Dexter leaves again or takes a sip of the lemonade and falls unconscious.

Nothing is interesting or out of the ordinary in here. Unless I had been interested in having a tie of every color. This guy truly is rich. I roll my eyes, picking up the craziest tie I see. It looks to be made of real gold, and by the surprising weight of it, I think it is. I admire its uselessness for a moment, moving to set it back into its spot.

Something behind it seems to be out of place—a panel in the wall that sticks out just a bit. I set the tie to the side, putting my hand over the strange square in the wall. It feels like metal, not concrete, as a wall should be. I explore it for a moment, discovering that I can move it to the side.

I lick my lips, finding a safe behind the sliding panel. Orson's expression is going to be priceless when he finds out that my mission wasn't a total failure. A blue screen blinks on, asking for a passcode. Let me see . . . this is a man of power. Not a total idiot, I'd assume. What would he use as his passcode?

I look at my watch to scan through Bree's research into Dexter Thomas's past. There are plenty of news stories, tabloid articles, and web pages. I try his birthday as the passcode, and it flashes red for a moment before reverting to blue. *Just great. This could take hours.* I try a few more things. His mother's birthdate, his cat's name, Poppy, and the name of his company, EarthKey, but nothing seems to work.

I hear Dexter's voice through the closet door. He seems to be on a phone call. I sit down, seeing nothing else to do. I have no choice but to wait for Luis to come to my rescue. Dexter's voice echoes through his empty throne room.

"Why, yes, Anna, I did see the newest report. EarthKey just gets more popular by the day. All you need to do now is keep my name in the headlines. Yeah. Thanks, Anna. Bye." He goes quiet. Dexter must have hung up the call. What a self-centered—

That's it. What would a billionaire love more than himself? He has no family, no friends, and ten thousand pictures of himself hanging on the way to his office. The file Luis showed me back at the precinct was filled with newspaper clippings that mentioned Dexter. There were pages and pages of his achievements, of clothing receipts, and transcripts from speeches. I flip through his file in my mind and remember a statement from a former secretary of Dexter's who went to court for a violation of the company's confidentiality policy. She had mentioned a code.

Oh.

After all, even if it doesn't work, it's worth a try. I type *DEXT* into the safe and it flashes green. I let out a breath as it swings open.

I start to dig through the safe, getting only a small, transparent screen out of it. I put it in my inner jacket pocket. I got what I came here for, and now I'm getting out of here, no matter if I have to fight tooth and nail for my escape. I walk out of the closet and look around the office.

The billionaire is slumped over his desk, his lemonade glass tipped over and pouring onto his dry-cleaned suit. I smirk, looking at my watch. I was informed that Luis would be here at 3:19 on the dot. I got everything I needed with one minute to spare. I wipe my forehead with my sleeve, feeling a little better.

Right on time, a techno-copter hovers by the floor-to-ceiling window, quietly floating. I walk over, clicking the panel on the wall. The window slides wide open and Luis smiles.

"I knew you could do it."

"I don't need your praise, Luis. I did my job. Now take this jerk to the police station where he belongs. And," I pull the screen out of my pocket, handing it to Luis, "make sure this goes with him. I think it's exactly what we need."

Luis nods, and I drag Dexter to the balcony, scooting a few cushioned chairs and ottomans out of my path with my foot. These past few weeks of training have helped me build strength, but he weighs about a hundred solid-gold ties. At least there's a positive side to being physically beaten in matches every day. I help Luis pull the man into the techno-copter and he slides the door shut. I watch as the copter disappears between two skyscrapers in the distance.

My foot taps at what feels like fifty miles an hour. If I walk out, the secretary will see me leave the office without his boss there. And I've run out of capsules to knock him out. *Great.* I look around for any other possible exits. This billionaire doesn't seem to have an emergency exit. There must be something. I look to the open window, walking over. Stepping onto the balcony, I see another from the floor below. Mom said I'd have an adventure . . . right?

CHAPTER 13

I've never had trouble with jumping fences. Just a climb and a jump. It's so easy. All you have to do is take a leap of faith. What's so different about a building thirty-four flights up? I can take a leap of faith, but whether I want to or not, this is my only way out.

Now, I'm not afraid of heights, but any sane adrenaline junkie would be afraid of free-falling without a parachute. I'm not crazy for not wanting to do this. I give myself the chance to find another escape, searching every inch of the room. The giant portrait of Dexter has hinges on the side. It could be his secret escape, but I see no way to open it. His computer shows no indication of a secret escape pod. I look for hidden buttons, switches, levers, or books that open the portrait when you pull on them. I find nothing. I even try to pry the painting open with my hands. No doubt guards will file into the office soon.

I put my palms on my forehead, laughing like a maniac. I start pacing, considering my options. Go out the obvious way, into the hall.

I'd have a chance of living but would definitely get caught. Or I climb down the side of a skyscraper. Guess which one I'm choosing.

I'd give anything for Orson to object right now, but he says nothing. Typical. When I need these people, they say nothing. I shake the sweat off my hands and grip the sides of the window frame. I look down at the ground, at the spot of concrete that is about to be on the news when I fall from this height.

Come on, Charlie. How else are you going to get home? I close my eyes tight, taking a few breaths. Letting go of the balcony's railing, I crouch and put my foot onto the ledge below, setting my other foot beside it. My hands turn white from my grip on the floor of the balcony above me.

A soft wind blows my hair into my face. Not exactly helpful at this moment. I slowly shift my feet inch by inch, my heels hanging over the edge. There must be a secret elevator or something that I'd missed. There's no way this is the escape plan for the creator of EarthKey.

I hold onto the ledge above with my fingertips. A bird flies by, taking a moment to inspect the oddity that is a sixteen-year-old girl climbing the outside of a skyscraper, thirty-four stories in the air. I glance below me, seeing a balcony with an open window on the floor directly below. I take a deep breath. This can't be too difficult.

Taking a leap of faith, I let go. The balcony catches my fall a few feet below me. I crouch down, holding onto the brick that lines the window ledge. My entire body trembles. I spend a moment hunched over, before climbing through the window. A plant I hadn't noticed tips over and smashes on the floor and I fall with it. I will myself to stand, my hair sticking to my sweat-covered face. This part doesn't seem as difficult. If only I didn't feel lightheaded. I remind myself every two seconds to stay awake.

It's a miracle no one's here. I'm in a break room with two doors— two possible exits. I pick the one on the left and find myself in a hallway with office doors on either side. Army-crawling, so as not to be seen through the office windows, I make it to the end of the hallway where a sign says "STAIRS" in white letters. I start to run down each flight, my heart pounding.

After what feels like an hour later, I take the final step and swing the ground floor door open. I cackle hysterically and stumble onto the sidewalk, running my hands through my ruined hair. Pedestrians' eyes glance toward me and I notice how crazy I must seem. I compose myself, starting to walk back to the precinct. I prepare an enraged speech the entire walk there, practicing my yelling in my mind.

I make it to the precinct, stomping past the sliding doors and into the lobby. Honey Adler's territory. The precinct is now a battlefield, and I will spare no survivors from my wrath. Faces turn to me. Luis, Honey, Orson, Bree, and others whose names I'd never cared to learn. They all stare, but I don't care how demented I look to them.

I glare at anyone who dares to make eye contact as Bree, Orson, and Luis make their way over to me. I slam my fist on the counter, and Honey nearly jumps out of her seat.

"Do you people know what I had to go through to get back here? I could have been killed!"

"Charlotte—"

"Don't 'Charlotte' me, Orson. And what was with going silent for over an hour with no explanation?"

"Charlie—"

"And you, Bree! Your false information could have gotten me shot. The documents were not on the computer! I had to find them myself."

"Charlie, you—"

"Luis, don't even get me started on you. Who has a techno-copter with only two seats? I thought this was a government organization! Who doesn't provide a copter with more seats?"

"CHARLIE!" Orson shouts, finally getting my attention. I stop my rant, watching the three of them. The expressions on their faces don't hold surprise, pride, or any form of anger. They just seem . . . sad. I look at Honey, who wipes her eye. Is she crying? What happened while I was gone?

"Is there something I need to know?" I watch them carefully, trying to pull any information I can out of them. Bree walks over, squeezing my arm. She gives me a pitying look.

"Maybe you should sit down for this."

Luis gravely pulls up a chair, motioning toward it. I watch him, sitting down.

"What's going on?" I brush my dirty palms onto my pants.

"Charlie," Orson says, watching me. "We got a report during your mission at EarthKey headquarters. About a death."

"Oh. Who died? Someone I know? From school?"

"Not quite." Bree sits beside me in a chair, putting her hand on my shoulder. I awkwardly move away, not understanding what they're trying to tell me.

"Don't sugarcoat it, Bree," Luis steps in. "We got a report about a murder. The victim's name was Ivy Starborne."

I stare at them. The world is blurry, and Bree mumbles something like, "I don't know how you feel, but we're here to help in any way we can," though I'm not paying attention. A chuckle escapes from my lips, and I stand, not noticing that I'm wobbling.

"You guys are really funny." I look at Luis, though I can't see him. I can tell I'm not crying, though.

"Charlie, we're sorry, but your mother . . . is dead."

I push past the bodies crowding me, stumbling. I stand in the middle of the lobby, staring at the ground. The memories of the past four weeks rush by frantically in my mind. The sleep deprivation, the bruises and cuts, the hours of coding and homework, the missions, the pain, and scaling a building.

A wave of exhaustion hits me, and my eyes shut, refusing to open. I collapse onto the floor. I can't move, but I don't care. Pain shoots through my body like I have been struck by lightning. My entire body trembles. Voices around me yell though I can't tell what they are saying. The floor is cold. The coldness soon fades away, and I'm numb.

Honey kneels beside me. "I know that this is hard to understand, but your mom is gone, Ms. Starborne. Just . . . talk to us. Please."

We got a report about a murder.

The victim's name was Ivy Starborne.

Your mother is dead.

Your mom is gone.

And then, I couldn't breathe.

CHAPTER 14

I need to escape. What a ridiculous thought. This is my destiny. To stay in this town until I die and eventually decompose. My roots have been planted and I'll never leave. No matter how much I want to. Not that it matters now. I don't care about leaving the city. I don't care about anything.

My mundane room glows with despair, the sun falling onto the walls. Their gray appearance only persuades me to stay in bed longer. There's no point in doing anything else. I should just stay here forever, watching the clouds roll by. The shining lives of outsiders reflect upon my sorrow.

My senses tingle. The house is filled with a soapy, clean smell. It doesn't smell anything like my home. *My* home always smelled like my mom's food, fresh out of the oven or off the stove. It must have been cleaned up after the murder. After all, who's going to want a house with a blood-stained carpet? My eyes sting at the thought.

"You need to get out. It's been three days," a deep voice calls from the doorway. I can only assume it's Orson.

"I was expecting a friendly face," my flat tone replies.

"Too bad," he says, moving closer. "You're getting me."

I stare at the ceiling, counting every second that Orson stays. The bed creaks as he sits on the side, and my skin burns under his gaze. There's no way I'm getting out of here without a speech. *Your mom died, but it's okay. I'm here.*

It's not okay. She died. I know. No one is trying to hide it. Not that they'd be able to do anything about it. She was murdered, and the precinct is so focused on the Dexter Thomas case that they couldn't care less. For some reason, Orson is here. I don't matter. Dexter Thomas doesn't matter. It's my mom that needs help. But these imbeciles can't do their job right, and we're stuck with no leads, no suspects, and no evidence.

Three and a half days. For three and a half days, I've been numb. I've never felt this way before, but it's peaceful. It's like sinking in quicksand. There's no escape, and fighting it will only make it worse. So, you give in to fate and vanish into darkness. And you're okay with it.

"You missed your congratulations party for the end of your sentence, Charlotte. We waited, then ended up canceling it. Not that we expected you to show up, but we thought there might still be a chance—"

"Stop talking, Bennet."

"When's the last time you ate?"

"It doesn't matter."

He studies my face but eventually realizes that he won't get any information out of me. I'm a closed book, stuck on the shelf. I'll just sit here, gathering dust.

"I need to talk to you."

"Aren't we talking right now?"

"We've contacted your father." This grabs my attention. My dad packed up his things the second he found out what I'd done. That wasn't the reason he left. It was his excuse. Last I heard, he was in Brazil living the bachelor life.

"He's not interested in taking you in." I can tell Orson is struggling with his words. He fixes the collar of his shirt, rests his elbows on his knees, and clasps his fingers together.

"Says he can't take on a kid in the house right now. It would be too much of a struggle." He sighs, fixing his collar once again. *Who would have known? My dad doesn't want me. It's not like I hadn't figured that out a year ago.*

"I bet you're wondering what's going to happen to you next, Charlie."

I'm not. I'm wondering how such a useless, stuck-up man could have been promoted to head of the precinct and then put on a project that wasn't going to help discover my mother's murderer. "Charlotte," he starts, "is there anyone you could contact? Someone in your family who we haven't heard of? Anyone?"

I narrow my eyes. "No."

"Well, that makes you an orphan," he says slowly, possibly hoping I'll comprehend. I can tell it hurts him to have this conversation with me, but it's not as if his comments can break my heart any more than it has already.

"What happens next?" I ask, actually wondering.

"I have made a call to Y-DOP," he coughs out, his voice resembling the smallest bit of a tremble.

I've heard of Y-DOP. Youth Deprived of Parents. Or as I like to say, dogcatchers for children. They chase down kids without supervision and throw them in a truck to be sent to what they call an "orphanage," though it's nothing of the sort.

The day after I agreed to join the EASY program team, Luis showed me a chart. As teen expectations increased, so did crime rates. The Justice Division was created to counteract the rising crime rate, as was Y-DOP. Keep kids off the streets, give them a meal, and they'll be less likely to break through a store window.

With the population decrease of the early 20s came an influx in the number of orphans. I was born in the mid-20s, so I don't remember a thing. Orphans are completely isolated from the society I grew up in. They live in Y-DOP's headquarters.

I had a friend, Hazel, who grew up in one of their facilities until a family adopted her online. From what she described, it was more like a mass jail. Nothing like the orphanages you'd see in a movie. But no one is there to stop them because the thing is, no one cares about orphans. They have no family, no one to contact.

Orson looks away from me. He stands after a moment, refusing to meet my eyes. I can feel my eyes pleading with him, though I can't sense a flicker of sadness behind them. He fixes his tie once more and hands me a notecard. On it is a time—3:00.

"They say they'll be coming over at 3:00 p.m. I'm sorry, but it's what's best. Goodbye, Charlie." He leaves me alone to ponder this information. Why would he give me the time? I recognize his reasoning. Orson wants me to escape. Make everyone think I went crazy and escaped so he could give me a chance to leave this dreaded town. I could leave. Start a new life, fake my age, get an apartment, start a job, maybe even find love. Be happy, get the life I've wanted.

I quickly stand, grabbing some clothes and my school bag. I look at my watch: 2:52 p.m. I have eight minutes to leave. Eight minutes to pack up my life. I gather a book about Socrates, a locket that holds a picture of me and my mother, and my digital cube. I toss them all onto my bed and search the house for more supplies.

A few granola bars are all the food I can find in the kitchen. The cabinets and fridge are filled with ingredients. We don't have leftovers. I rush into my mother's room. I look around for a moment. Her bed is neatly made, as always, and her digital cube sits on the nightstand. A small holo-screen in the corner plays a looped slideshow, pictures of us appearing, then disappearing, on the screen. Almost like she never left. *Almost.*

I shake the thought of taking any of her things and grab the small holo-screen. Her drawer is slightly open, and I dig through it. I find an ID and a money card. I lick my lips, head back to my bed, and shove everything into my schoolbag. I check my watch again: 2:57.

I sling the bag over my shoulder and go to the back door, which hasn't been opened in years. It's old with hinges, so I've ignored it. My mom and I once tried to have a garden, but that didn't work out well, and we forgot the backyard even existed. The door won't budge. My watch tells me the time is 2:58.

I prop my foot up on the wall, putting all of my strength and weight into opening the door. It still won't move, and my arm aches. The pain medication I've been taking every day after sparring with Luis ran out yesterday. I start to hear noises—small, but powerful, voices from the front of the house. I glance at the door again and sigh loudly. I was pulling the door when it should be pushed. I turn the handle and slam my body against the wood. Pain shoots through my body, but the door swings open. *Success.*

I tear through the brewing storm. Rain has yet to start, but the dark clouds portend what's coming. The climate isn't the only thing changing. My ears perk up as the SWAT team for children bursts through the locked front door of what used to be my house.

My former house. I cringe at the thought. I've been betrayed by the only people I could have ever trusted. There is no more precinct, no home, no friends, no allies, no family. Just me and this bag I now must lug around. But it's not the only thing that weighs me down.

I carry my heavy bag and my heavy heart through the unforgiving wind.

CHAPTER 15

Betrayal. That's the perfect word for it. Betrayed by my mind, by the precinct, and now by my feet. My shoes can only carry me so far, and I can only run for so long before someone will find me. It won't be long, especially since the city has kept tabs on me in the past. I sit on the edge of a chipped piece of the sidewalk, examining my surroundings.

Pinewood Alley. *Who's going to look for me here?* It's a worn-down neighborhood that is home to convicts, pickpockets, and people who swear to have spotted UFOs. The buildings around here were graffitied and broken into so much that businesses just packed up and left. Now the abandoned area is worth almost nothing, and people released from jail can live here directly after their sentences. I've heard that many have tried to find jobs and get out, but most are stuck here forever. It's kind of sad, but the city pays them no attention. That's exactly why it's perfect for me, with Y-DOP searching for me and no place to call home.

I'm too lost in thought to notice a woman rushing up to me.

"Hello," she says, scaring the living hell out of me, "Charlotte, is it?"

I look her up and down. She is a round woman with gray hair pulled into a low ponytail. Her eyes are a beautiful amber, a liquid gold sea in an archipelago of freckles.

I mentally prepare myself to run, when suddenly her face softens.

"Oh! Oh dear, I've scared you. Don't be afraid. I have a place where you can hide."

I'm about to ask her how she knew my name when she turns a corner. I quickly follow. We head into a smaller building, the door sliding open at our arrival. The woman continues through a door across the room. I don't trust going farther into the building than I already have, so I stay in what looks like a lobby.

The place smells of rotting fruit, and the floor creaks as I take a few steps forward to examine the peeling wallpaper. I start to hear chatter coming from a lit doorway. Though I promised I wouldn't go any further, this spikes my curiosity, and I advance slowly and quietly, in an attempt to listen in. My aching feet fail me. The chatter stops. I freeze.

What's the worst they could do to me? Should I fight them off? Am I strong enough? I toss my options back and forth, never thinking of hiding. The same woman opens the door and smiles. Behind her is a little boy with hair that looks like it hasn't been combed in a week. His baby blue eyes embody the same beauty. They are somehow familiar.

The third face that emerges is one I recognize. A man of around nineteen or twenty, who carries himself with pride and grace. Luis. His first reaction is a smile. I stand there like a fool. My curiosity gets the better of me sometimes. It plants my feet on the wrong ground at the wrong times.

Luis speaks. "Charlotte, I was so worried. Orson told me that he contacted Y-DOP, and I thought you'd, well," he says, pausing to glance at the smaller boy as if to guard the boy's innocence. "I just didn't want you to get hurt, is all. I completely disagree with everything Y-DOP does. My family and I have saved as many kids as we can." He nods to the woman and the boy standing beside him. The woman gives a small wave.

I blink, confused. "Family? These people are—"

"Did you think I was alone?"

"No, I guess I just never thought about it. About you. Your life." I quickly realize my mistake. I was ignorant, only thinking of myself. Of course Luis has a family. That's one difference between us. I shake myself out of the thought, closing my eyes.

As if reading my mind, Luis puts a hand on my shoulder, causing me to look up. "Let me introduce you. This is my aunt, Iris, and my little brother, Theodore." They smile.

I break my gaze from the named strangers, looking back to Luis. "Do you—I'm sorry. Do you live here?" He doesn't seem offended. I bet he gets this look of pity all the time.

Luis tucks a hand into his pocket, not answering. His non-verbal cue gives me the answer I need. Previously working a desk job, tirelessly trying to get the EASY program on its feet, the purple circles under his eyes, and groggy responses to questions; I missed all the signs. He overworks himself, obviously for his family.

People today aren't known to put in as much effort into their jobs as they did years ago, especially after the crash of '08 when most were working to recharge the economy. Now, most expect a robot or AI to do the work for them. You can get the work done with a few clicks, then sit back and watch your handy AI friend bring cash in for you. The only ones known to do actual work are the ones who are living in poverty. They can't depend on AI. The demand is too high, and it's too expensive. Ever since self-dependent Artificial Intelligence flew into the market, companies recognized its popularity and started overpricing everything. Families like Luis' are lucky to get a phone with a simple holographic ask-and-response program.

"Looking for a place to run to?" Luis' eyes examine mine, but he knows the answer to that question.

"Maybe," is all I can spit out. "Or maybe I'm taking a simple stroll around town."

"Well, you didn't have to sound so sarcastic about it," Theodore remarks. This shocks me, not only because I forgot Luis' family was there, but because I was unaware that such a blunt comment could come from someone as young as Theodore. The statement doesn't seem to faze Iris or Luis. I assume this is normal for them.

"Charlotte, don't worry, we've got you covered," Luis nods reassuringly.

A few minutes later, there is a ragged blanket with a matching pillow set up on a stage. Literally. A stage. Theodore informs me that this building—their home—used to be a small community theater before the municipality decided it had been driven into the ground by hooligans. It's precisely my luck that Luis' family would find me.

Theodore seems to be talkative, giving me answers to questions I hadn't asked and talking over the questions I do ask. He is the complete opposite of Iris, who has barely spoken since our first encounter. Iris leaves to give me some space, and Luis goes to make a phone call. Theodore stays behind, his cheeks glowing with questions. I tell him to go distract himself with a toy or digital cube and he responds that he doesn't have any devices.

I really need to teach myself to shut up. Luis is poor, and I'm a jerk, and everything is a mess. My eyes fall to the floor.

I assume he gets the message from my sad demeanor because he eventually excuses himself to his room.

I am now alone, on a stage, in Pinewood Alley. This is not how I thought my week would go, to be honest. I'd rather not think about the negative, but it seems to be an impossible task to disregard depressing thoughts. It's not every day you are told, "Hey! Guess what? You're an orphan now. Here's a one-way ticket to Nowhere, USA." It's hard to process, and while some could say I'm in shock or denial, I think I'm just exhausted.

So exhausted. Honestly, I'm the most exhausted I've ever been. Sleep has been a distant concept to me these past few days. Now it seems to settle my mind. It's nice to have an internal escape. Relaxing.

I take one last look around this musty, damp theater, and find myself admiring the building. In my fatigue, I can only imagine the plays that could have been performed here. *Macbeth, Death of a Salesman, The Wizard of Oz* . . . It reminds me of a quote I had to memorize for my Literature class. A simple line from Shakespeare's *Henry VI.* It meant nothing to me back then, but now, it seems to mean the world:

To weep is to make less the depth of grief.

My back touches the hardwood floor of the stage, and I pull the ruined, yet comforting, blanket over me. Shakespeare's line replays in my mind, though I cannot seem to search for a reason why it holds such importance. Here I am, lying on an actual stage, and I can't think of an explanation of its meaning.

It might simply be the exhaustion, but I swear it must mean something. I stare up at the grid above the stage and the darkness envelops me as sunset comes to an end. For a moment, before the sun disappears, I swear the velvet seats of the theater glow a soft honey-gold.

To weep is to make less the depth of grief. What an eerie line to have stuck in my head. I lie here in the black of night, my mind washed of any thought but the one repeating excerpt. I gradually doze off, the line's intensity fading with my consciousness. I drift out of this world, the quote now gone. But a single question stands firm as I finally sleep for the first time in days.

If all the world's my stage, is there a way to change the story?

CHAPTER 16

Blinding sunlight filters through my bedroom window as I start packing for school. My bag is almost packing itself. I walk downstairs and yell my goodbye to my mom, stepping out the front door. My feet crunch on the rocks of the pavement, and the May clouds pass me by, smoothly changing shape as they travel.

I know somewhere in the back of my mind this isn't real. It can't be. Am I hallucinating? Dreaming? I pinch myself and feel nothing. Yep, I'm definitely dreaming. Realizing where I am, my eyes widen. I will myself to turn back to my house. To turn back to my life. To mom. But my legs force me to keep moving. I know I'm dreaming and that I'm not in control. Like fish in a Herculean current, all I can do is follow along and see how this plays out.

The school comes into view, and storm clouds replace the fluffy, white ones in the blink of an eye. It is not morning now, but night. A honeyed voice speaks behind me. I recognize it immediately, whirling around.

"Ready, Lotta?"

There is only one person who has dared to call me Lotta in my life. I meet Noah's eyes, glaring. His cheek bears a bruise, his lip is split, and his right eye is swollen shut. I remember this day. I wish I didn't remember it.

"Of course I'm ready. Don't you know me?" I reply with a smirk, though it's not me saying those words.

He chuckles, an awful sound to my ears now, though I'd loved everything about it back then. We were close friends, but I had a little bit of a crush on him. Noah grabs my hand and we run to the back of the school. I mimic his steps with a wicked grin stretching across my face.

I mentally scold myself for the actions of the old me, annoyed that I have to relive every moment now. Noah takes his backpack in one hand, flinging it off his shoulder. I hold onto my backpack with one hand, watching him as he digs through the compartment where his e-books and tablet should be. But of course, schoolwork is the last thing on Noah's mind. He gets a small badge out, and I recognize it as that of a school janitor.

Noah swipes the employee's badge on the scanner and it slides open as we enter the dreary, clean building. The door leads us to the science classroom, which is known for having no surveillance. Noah throws a pair of leather gloves at me. I slide them on, watching as he gets his laptop out to hack the school cameras and shut them off. This takes about fifteen minutes, which I know by impatiently checking my watch. He slides on his pair of gloves and nudges my shoulder.

"Get the matches from Mrs. Griffin's desk, then meet me at the locker," Noah says before strolling out. I walk to the desk where I pick the lock on the drawer. This is no new task. Noah took me on adventures like this one often. But this one seems different. More dangerous. It didn't faze me at the time, but looking back, all I want to do is shake myself by the shoulders and scream sense into my empty head.

After a few seconds of searching through the teacher's desk, I find the matchbox and lock the drawer once again. My feet softly hit the marble floor as I rush to the location of the soon-to-be crime. Noah is leaning against the wall, standing in his usual "cool guy" pose. I have it burned into my head by now. One hand in his back pocket, one foot propped between the wall and the floor. And who could forget his signature one-hand-behind-the-neck move? I'm smarter now and find it utterly repulsive.

"Got the jug? And the matches?" he asks, his sandy eyes searching mine. Well, one eye. His other is still unable to open. I wish I'd been the one that punched him.

I nod, getting the evidence out of my backpack. One jug of gasoline, and a paper with the locker's code on it. I set the gasoline and match on the floor, read the code, and type it into the locker. It swings open. Noah smiles. An evil smile. A smile like a waning crescent moon. The smile fades, turning into a gruesome scowl.

"Ethan's going to be sorry. No one humiliates me. He needs to learn," he says.

"Luckily, he has you to teach him," I remark. His smile returns.

I remember Ethan. A rich, annoying guy the same age as me, who had bullied Noah until he snapped. After Noah had refused to steal the semester exam from the algebra teacher's classroom, Ethan and his buddies found Noah during lunch and did a real number on him. I wince at the thought of the beatdown.

Noah decided he needed my help to get back at his bully. He wanted to scare Ethan but didn't want anyone to get seriously hurt. Noah had quickly called to catch me, his best friend, up on the plan. Noah was thoughtful in that way and only that way. He would never hurt a fly. At least, that's what I thought at the time.

I was to meet him at school that night with the code to Ethan's locker—which had been sold to me for a fair price—a jug of enough gasoline to light a noticeable fire, and the matches from Mrs. Griffin's desk, which I had seen the day before when I asked her for a pencil. The plan would work like a charm. No cameras, no fingerprints, no evidence, but the message was sure to get to Ethan. And if Ethan ratted us out, he would be reprimanded for hurting a student.

"Lotta, get the matches ready," Noah says, pouring gasoline over the inside of Ethan's locker. Ethan's school tablet crackles, the liquid breaking the device. Once he steps back, it's my turn. He steps a few feet away from the locker and I do the same, lighting the match. I try to stop my old self from throwing it, screaming for help. But it's no use. The dream refuses to let me speak. All I can do is stand here, watching through my younger self's eyes.

The match flies into the locker and lands on the now-broken tablet. In less than a second, the locker is engulfed in flames. The lockers surrounding it also suffer, their paint melting off. I glance at Noah, whose eyes are smoldering with an evil passion. This isn't right, but the old me smirks as if it's the most moral thing she could be doing.

This isn't me. Not anymore.

I hate what happens next. After a few moments of watching the locker burn, Noah grabs his backpack and takes off, his shoes pounding against the floor. My head snaps to watch him, confused and stunned. I take one more glance at the locker's paint, peeling in the blaze. My feet follow his.

Noah runs through the door we entered through, slamming it behind him. It locks automatically, a precaution created after a school in Indiana figured out they could catch students, or criminals, committing crimes in schools by trapping them in the building after school hours. Noah has a stolen janitor's badge, so he can come and go as he pleases. I, however, do not have a badge and am stuck in the building.

"Noah, what's going on?" I yell through the door.

"Someone's gotta get caught for setting a fire on school property. It won't be me!" he yells back. A year ago, I couldn't believe this. My crush on Noah blocked any bit of sense I may have had in my brain. I would have done almost anything for him, but not this. Not go to jail.

"Noah, please, don't do this," I find myself pleading, hitting the door as he watches with what looks like pure joy. I have no idea why I had fallen for someone so sadistic. "Let me out of here. We can frame someone else!" My voice grows louder but it has no effect on Noah. I still remember the last thing he'd said to me.

"Don't act so innocent here, Lotta. You committed a crime. Set a school locker on fire without hesitation. So who's the real bad guy here?" His serious face turns into another one of his evil smiles. "Promise me you'll call from behind bars. Thanks for being here for me. I really needed you. You're such a good friend," Noah says, walking away.

The building's fire alarm system goes off, creating a deafening noise and alerting authorities. A robot will extinguish the flame and the school will be okay, but the damage can't be undone. I'm grateful for the alarm's volume because it muffles my sobs.

My heart cannot tolerate reliving this event. My stupidity, Noah, Ethan, the locker, the fire, the matches in Mrs. Griffin's desk, the janitor's security badge, all of it. Though I can't handle what happens next, I remember it perfectly. I remember every second of this day and the two weeks that followed it.

Right on cue, sirens blare in the distance.

CHAPTER 17

It's been a week since Luis gave me a home. I explore the theater and some of the buildings around it every day. The other inhabitants leave me alone as they travel to their lives in the outside world. Iris goes to work at the nearby grocery store, Theodore attends school, and Luis goes to the precinct. He tells me to keep a low profile, and that's exactly what I do. A week has gone by, and, to my knowledge, no one is looking for me.

Pinewood Alley is peaceful. It seems everyone who lives on the block wants a quiet life where they can hide out, like me. The streets are mostly quiet, and small groups mill around, disappearing into buildings that have been repurposed, used as houses, bars, stores, and barbershops. The tranquility makes the block a wonderful place to think, but all I can think about is the dream from last night. After the court handed me my sentence, I thought I'd never have to face Noah again. I never expected to see him in a dream.

Nevertheless, things in Pinewood are easier. Even with my fears of seeing Noah again, in a dream or real life, I manage. This life is far better than the one I was living before. It's free. I have no need to worry about homework, jerks snickering behind my back, or having to show up at the precinct every day. After I completed my sentence, and Luis helped me enroll in homeschool, everything just seems to have a simpler answer. Though there is one thing I miss.

I blink away the thought. It hurts too much to think about my mom. To remember that I couldn't attend her funeral while in hiding. Luis told me it was a beautiful ceremony and that he left a bouquet of roses, her favorite, in my absence.

"Morning, Charlie," a voice says, startling me. I turn around to face Luis. My muscles relax.

He walks past me, getting a mug from a tall cabinet in the theater's kitchen. Luis' decision to live in an abandoned theater is genius. It has plenty of rooms, a few large bathrooms, and a functional kitchen. Luis fills the mug with coffee, watching me. I've learned by now that he expects me to say something.

"Uh, good morning." I'd usually throw in a snarky remark, but I don't feel the need to defend myself against Luis anymore.

He smiles, taking a sip from his cup of coffee. "I'm headed to the precinct. Iris already dropped Theodore at school, and she shouldn't be back from work for about seven hours. Have fun."

I know the drill, but I don't understand why Luis feels the need to explain his family's routine to me every morning. I keep quiet about it, as I do with every other annoyance. The last thing I need is to be on the streets.

Luis tosses out a "goodbye" before heading out the door. I watch him go, then make my way to the stage, my personal space. It's clean for a place so old. I'd say it was almost beautiful. Right at noon every day, the sun's position strikes the golden-velvet box seats hanging ten feet over the stage, making them glow.

I climb to the catwalk to get a view of the perfect, shimmering space below me. Maybe in a different time or universe, I would have loved the theater. I could have been a tech expert or stage manager. In a different universe, I could have even performed.

My head snaps up when I hear yelling from inside the building. Theodore, Iris, and Luis are all gone, and they wouldn't make this much noise, even if they were back. Crashes bring the space to life. I duck below the catwalk's handrail to hide from whatever dangers may be making all the noise.

I hold my breath as the monstrous sounds crawl closer. The double doors swing open, my worst fears coming true. A group of three men and one woman scatter in different directions, surveying the area. They're looking for something. Me.

I recognize these government-issued outfits immediately. The clothes are Y-DOP's signature. Dove-white, business-casual suits that make the agents look like they are returning from a board meeting. The suits are meant to maintain the professional image of the government-funded company yet be flexible enough to chase down children. They are made with a special FBI-developed fabric. An advanced piece of technology that can manipulate a person's movements and help in a fight. The army uses a similar fabric.

The supercomputer that's embedded in the suit uses a camera to analyze potential situations and work out how to react to them. If I were to fight the Y-DOP agents, they would easily win. The suit would predict any kick, punch, or movement I could make, and it would respond to neutralize me immediately.

Y-DOP agents seem almost inhuman. The suits make them stronger and faster than any other person. I am outnumbered, out-planned, and outgunned. I wish I were able to afford a cool suit like theirs, or a decent weapon, but it's impossible.

The terrifying agents stealthily move through each aisle of seats, looking for any clue of an inhabitant. I wonder what led them to me. They have already searched through my small setup on the stage and have started to explore the large backstage area. I examine them for a moment, slowly creeping across the catwalk as I do. I can't risk being seen or heard.

I feel like prey stalking the predator, knowing that they could find me and pounce at any moment. A stream of hope flows through me as I notice a small door behind the back curtain of the theater. *An escape.* All that stands between me and freedom is an old metal ladder.

My feet press firmly into the rungs of the ladder to try to prevent the rusty metal from creaking. The Y-DOP agents stop sneaking around, whispering to each other through earpieces. They sneak out of the theater, and I take a much-needed breath of relief.

I finish climbing down the ladder and rush out the back door. I can come back later for my things if the Y-DOP agents haven't taken them.

I freeze in my tracks at the sight of a white Y-DOP van waiting for me outside.

They knew I would find the escape. They decided to chase me out of the back door, right into their arms. My heart pounds in my ears and my eyes brim with tears.

Come on, Charlie. Now isn't the time to act weak. I do the only thing I can think of, pouncing on the first Y-DOP employee I see. My fist swings through the air, aiming for their face. The suit reacts, catching my arm. My knees feel like jelly.

The Y-DOP agents surround me, creating a circular wall that blocks any escape. I remember my training from the precinct and use every move that comes to mind. It makes no difference. These people are too strong for me. I am outnumbered.

One of them—with the name Edwards imprinted on her suit—takes out a small, glass block with a blue power surge glowing at the center. Edwards presses it to my neck and a terrible shock goes through me. I assume it would have knocked me out immediately if they wanted it to, but it sends me to the ground, paralyzed.

They set me on a flat, padded bench in the van. Other than that, it is just as empty as its outside makes it seem, besides a few fold-down chairs attached to the wall. A shot is administered into my arm, though I can hardly feel it over the ice-cold pain running down my back. My cheek feels wet. It must be either tears or blood. I can't tell the difference.

I start to lose consciousness as the Y-DOP agents climb into the van, sitting in chairs across from me. Plastic straps buckle over the agents, and they stare forward at the wall. I can only hear the beginning of the conversation two of the agents have.

"Is she going to the education center like the rest of them?" One says.

"No, Bill. Our orders are to take Starborne to Bree Pierces," the other replies. "They must know one another. Ms. Pierces never asks for guests."

Now, where have I heard that name before?

CHAPTER 18

Well, this is the definition of a setback. I'm waiting in a small room, one arm chained to the chair I'm sitting in to ensure I won't run. Why am I here, and what does Bree have to do with any of this? Is she a double agent?

The room is lit by the large skylight above me, and a fern sits in the corner. A gray desk sits across from me, with a white, Y-DOP-issued swivel chair behind it. The desk has a glass top, resembling the one Dexter Thomas had in his office. It must be a holographic screen. Whatever they're doing here, it's secret.

The door behind me whooshes open. I tense, glaring at the digital clock in front of me. It's 3:19. I was knocked out for a few hours if that clock is reliable. When I woke up, I was in a stark-white room with a single, metal door and a sink in the corner. I was about to go crazy until they called me into this office, about half an hour later. That must be who this is. Bree Pierces, the traitor.

The pale girl fixes her glasses, sitting in the seat behind the desk. I turn my glare to her. She bites her lip nervously, throwing me a smile after a moment. This throws me off. I was expecting something that mirrored the dirty look I was giving her.

"Hey, Bree," I say through clenched teeth.

"Charlie, it's nice to see you again. We've been wondering where you were," Bree says, leaning comfortably back in her chair. "Orson, Luis, and I were hoping you were safe."

I smirk slightly, sitting up. "That's funny because I've been with Luis for over a week. And Orson is the one who gave me the chance to run." Her face reddens, and I continue. "It seems you were out of the loop. Do you mind taking these handcuffs off now?"

"Charlotte, we need to talk," Bree says, then stands to step around the desk. She sits on the edge, just a few feet in front of me. I maintain my glare. "As you may have figured out by now, I work with Y-DOP. Well, not just me. The team at the precinct has allied with Y-DOP."

I stare. My confusion slowly changes to anger, and I try to leap at Bree, but I'm yanked back by the handcuffs.

"You're working with these monsters?" I spit out. "Do you know what these people do? They take government checks and treat the kids here like garbage! This isn't a home for orphaned children, it's a prison. They're helpless, and it's overlooked because no one cares about orphans. There's no one *to* care for them." I notice now that I'm crying, but I keep going. "*No one cares.* Y-DOP could kill these kids, and no one would bat an eye."

Bree seems unfazed by my plea. She must hear this all the time. She gives me a moment to compose myself, but once she realizes that I can't stop crying, she starts to give her side of the argument.

"Charlie, these kids are orphaned, yes. But think about how they became orphans. Some were abandoned by their parents, some come from families on the wrong side of the tracks, some are runaways, some have parents that passed away due to the global virus, and some were abused or have parents that were killed. Like you."

I look up. Bree gives me a sad smile, continuing. "These kids have been neglected, abused, and are *witnesses* to many crimes." She winks at me, hinting. I narrow my eyes.

"Are you seriously suggesting—"

"Creating a mass version of the EASY program, putting kids under, scouring their memories for undiscovered criminals? I think you're catching on."

Bree is smart, sure, but that doesn't mean she can convince me to throw away my morals. It makes me think of Mr. Ariosto's class. Would he want me to use these kids for the benefit of others? We'd be throwing them in interrogation rooms, looking through their memories, making them dive into their pasts.

"You can't seriously be considering exploiting Y-DOP's children just to add to your count of how many crimes you've solved."

"It's not exploiting. We're helping them and helping *society*. The world needs our help. Wasn't that the first thing Luis taught you? The government's restructuring has given us a fresh start. A chance to fix things. Through the EASY program, we can save so many lives, and get justice for so many who have not received it. This could be beautiful." Bree stares off into the distance as if imagining her utopia. "People like you—"

"I'm not like them. Don't paint me as a victim," I say, my voice nearly shattering.

"Right, of course. But think of it. If we could solve your mother's murder, along with solving the cases of thousands of others, we could make a change. A real impact."

I consider this. Solving my mom's murder? I wish I knew who killed her. I'd do the same injustice to them as they had done to her just over a week ago.

"Bree . . . where are your parents?"

"They would be proud of me, Charlie."

"Where are they?" The heels of my shoes dig into the solid floor. I wish I could sink through, leave, and start with a clean slate, but that option drifts further away each time I open my mouth.

The teen's eyes shimmer. "My mother passed away when I was two. My father was nothing if not transparent. He told me every detail in the hopes that I would remember her in her last years. The virus of the '20s was almost gone when the world started to rebuild. Most were immune, but my mother—let's just say her immune system wasn't the most agreeable. She survived the virus's worst waves. Then one day she couldn't stop sneezing. She ran a fever. It wasn't so bad. Not until her cheeks turned near purple and her hearing faded. My father didn't want to believe it so he convinced her to stay home. Rest. Avoid the doctor's office. It wasn't until two weeks later, when my dad was at a luncheon, that her throat closed up. They couldn't save her."

"So you have your dad?"

"Not quite, Charlie." Bree spins a metal pen on the desk and watches as it slows to a stop. "My father raised me well. But as the years went by, and I turned five, then six, then seven, he started to avoid eye contact. He spoke less." She stared off into space. "I found a picture of my mother in his desk drawer once. We had the same nose, the same eyes. I suspect it hurt him too much to look at me. But he didn't have to live with me long. On my eighth birthday, Y-DOP took me in. I don't know what happened to him, but I never asked. I made connections and built myself up the corporate ladder from there. With a few agreements and exceptions, I was released into society at eleven."

The room is as loud as a still tundra.

"What happened to you? Why traumatize kids like us?" I finally say.

"I'm not sure what you mean. I am *not* the villain here, Charlotte. *Society* is. We let criminals run rampant until they're caught, and many never are. But here, this idea, *my* idea—we can start taking preventive measures. More statistics, more data, but with fewer risks. Those children will just have to . . . take one for the team. But in the long run, isn't that what's truly best? Sacrifice a few, help a world."

"Do Orson and Luis know about this?" I ask.

She watches me for a moment, calculating what to say next.

"No," she finally says, "they don't know. But they will soon. It's a brilliant idea, and I need you on board."

I thought of saying the words I'd said over a month ago at the precinct when they wanted to recruit me. I thought of responding "I'll do it," and compromising my morals once again. I thought I was helping–going out on a limb and using the EASY program to catch criminals.

Now I know that Bree is taking it too far. First, it's suspects, previous offenders, and untrustworthy psychopaths, but next it'll be victims and kids who don't know any better. The EASY program was being run by an anxious, demented, eighteen-year-old girl. Behind those glasses was a monster.

"Y-DOP is going to help many, many people," Bree says, sitting back in her chair.

I can't breathe. I remember her words now. *What's one person's memory when you could save hundreds?* Why didn't I see it before?

"Society really failed you, Bree," I manage to say. "You're young and intelligent. And I'm going to stop you."

Bree smiles slightly. I know the most terrifying thing is that she doesn't realize what she's doing is wrong. She has no idea about the pain she's going to inflict on all of these children. Bree is a villain.

"No, you won't. I'm sorry for what has to happen next." She presses the corner of the desk, speaking to it. "Rhig, please take Charlotte Starborne to the education center."

I perk up, staring at her. "Bree, no. Please."

Bree swivels the chair around, staring at the clock on the wall. She doesn't want to listen to me. A bulky man with a crooked nose walks in and unlocks the handcuff attached to the chair. He does this carefully, so as not to hurt me, but he is obviously very strong.

The man seizes my arm to walk me out. I say nothing, knowing that it will do no good. He takes me into a glass elevator, pressing a button that glows blue at his touch. The elevator starts to shoot down, and I look up at him. He's about two feet taller than me and much more muscular.

"So, are you Rhig?" I ask, trying to distract myself. He doesn't respond, looking forward. He must do this all the time. It seems like just another duty for him. A company badge hangs from his neck, and

I lean closer, squinting to read it. Annoyed, he pushes me away, but not before I can read his badge.

Rhig Sanders. Forty-one. A loyal member of Y-DOP for thirty-two years. It's normal for bigger organizations to include age and work information to better organize their employees, but something's not right.

I blink a few times, looking forward at the floors passing by. A member for thirty-two years? That means he was working here at nine, but that's impossible. Unless—

"So, you've been here for a while, huh?" I say as we step off the elevator, having reached Sublevel 1.5, an underground level between two floors. I would learn afterward the .5 floors are the housing units of the education center.

"You've been here for a long time?" I repeat. Rhig doesn't seem in the mood for answering questions, though that might just be what his face usually looks like. We move through the bleak hallway; silver benches every ten yards. There are white, tall panels on both sides as we make our way to my new prison. I figure out that these panels are high-security doors, made to keep the kids in order.

Rhig pushes me into my room and the door slides shut behind me. The room is suffocating, the size of a walk-in closet, and has a twin bed in the center. It has a room in the back, which I think is the bathroom, and a box in the wall, which, through further inspection, turns out to be a dumbwaiter for food and other necessities.

I realize how exhausted I am. I lie down, staring at the gray ceiling above me. Luis will come home and think I've run away again. He'll worry, but after a while, he'll forget about it.

I'm going to rot here.

CHAPTER 19

After about a month at Y-DOP, I start to get the hang of things. I get a student badge that hangs around my neck everywhere I go. I only leave the underground floors for *kinesthetic activities* twice a day.

The schedule is very straightforward, and I memorize it quickly. First, breakfast arrives through the dumbwaiter in the wall. Next, a panel on the wall in your room displays the Y-DOP news. Mostly propaganda about how they're *helping children to grow to their full potential* and junk like that. A few times a week, there will be a segment or two on a child trying to escape and facing the consequences.

After that, we have sixteen minutes to shower, dress, and brush our teeth. We can walk the floor whenever we want, unless school is in session or a mandatory activity is happening. School is private for each Y-DOP child. It's a lot like homeschool, but we have 10-minute breaks every hour when we can order a snack. The setup isn't that bad. I fall into rhythm with the other kids and enjoy that, for once, the pressure is being lifted from my shoulders.

The rest of the day is various activities, some mandatory, and then time to yourself. The only social time we get is during kinesthetic activities or walking around in the hallway, but I find that I like the silence. It gives me more time to think of my escape plan. And when I get bored of silence, I listen to music through my ceiling speaker or watch Y-DOP-approved movies on the wall panel.

The news on other kids attempting escape has taught me what not to do. I take notes in a school notebook that I keep under my pillow. I'm not stupid enough to write the plans in the Notes app on my Y-DOP-issued computer.

I finally figure out the floor situation. Every floor has three supervisors. Mine are two women, whose names I haven't bothered to learn, and Rhig. In the past month, I have earned Rhig's trust. It works like this:

"Morning, Rhig," I say with a bright smile.

"Mornin' Charlotte. What'd you get today?" he says, returning the smile.

"Raspberry muffin. Hasn't changed all month. But hey, I'm not hungry anyway. You take it."

"Really?"

"Yeah," I hand him the muffin every morning, and every morning he practically skips down the hall, smiling from the gesture.

Then in the afternoon:

"Rhig, I can't stay in this place anymore," I say, tears streaming from my face. I'd learned to keep my eyes open for two minutes to stimulate tears.

"You can do this, Charlotte. You're strong. You remind me of my daughter, Frieda," he says, pushing a tissue box across the table in the common room.

Then later:

"I miss my dad so much. And my friends. And my school." All untrue, but Rhig eats it up like candy, comforting me.

It's all a part of the plan. I gain a supervisor's trust, like Rhig, then knock him out somehow, steal his badge, and make my way to sweet, sweet freedom. I'll admit that it's not the most thought-out plan, but it's all I've got. One screw-up and there will be no chance of me getting out, ever. This place is suffocating.

Today, during kinesthetic activities, I sit on a bench to the side and talk to Rhig. Though I'm just using his caring spirit for my own benefit, I've actually found him to be a great listener. He's the only person I've talked to here.

"So, when you were nine," I start.

"My father was shot in an armed robbery at his favorite grocery store," he says, finishing my thought. "My mom was so devastated. She always called him her soulmate." Rhig takes a deep breath, clenching the edges of the bench until his knuckles turn pale. "She died three months later of a broken heart. Well, that's what I was told. I think it was cancer, though."

"And Y-DOP took you in."

"I signed up willingly. They didn't have to run after me."

I nod, looking down at my silver-painted nails. I took a trip to the recreation room earlier and got my first manicure ever. They really want this place to seem more like a hotel than a high-security prison for minors. But Rhig has been a friend. Maybe I can trust him, just this once, in return for his trust.

"Rhig, I'm going to be honest," I say, watching the kids in the kinesthetic area run on treadmills or play with toy cars. "This place is a prison with nicer water fountains."

He chuckles in his raspy voice. "I agree."

"Really?" I look at him. "Then why continue to work here?"

"You think staying is my choice?" He looks at me. I can tell by the seriousness in his eyes that he's not joking. "I thought coming here would be a good idea, but I had no idea they'd try to keep me. Tried to escape eight times in my childhood. I didn't know what I was in for. Three tacks and they put you in Isolated Care. After a few months in Isolated Care, ya go back to the normal floors. But when they decided I was causing too much trouble, they kept me down there for half a year. One day, a Y-DOP agent walked in and—" he gulps as he pauses.

"What?" I ask, actually invested in his story.

"Well, the agent told me they'd let me out of Isolated Care for good if I signed a contract that, well, gave them permission to keep me working here for life. So I became a member instead of a student."

"Where are the kids in Isolated Care?"

"Sublevel 5. After two times in Isolated Care, they came with the contract, and I was free. Well, more free than before. I can go outside whenever I like now."

"And what's Sublevel 5 like?" I move closer, trying to get back on topic.

"It's terrible. You don't get kinesthetic activities or a recreation center. You can't even leave your room in your free time. And there are small focus groups where you talk about your feelings to the rest of the Y-DOP kids in Isolated Care. Like therapy, kinda."

"That does sound terrible," I say, and I mean it.

Rhig stands at the *ding* that signals us to go back to our rooms. It sounds like the bell at school, but with a menacing undertone. Like ants in a line, the Y-DOP slaves file back into the elevators and their rooms.

"I just wish I could stop all of this craziness. I wish I could get you out of here for good," I ponder out loud, and I mean it.

We wait for everyone to file out of the room, then enter an empty elevator. Rhig scans his badge on the elevator wall. I look up at him, raising an eyebrow, but say nothing. Unless a Y-DOP member scans their badge and orders it to go somewhere else, the elevators automatically go to the housing floors from the recreation room.

Rhig presses a button on the wall. We start to move upward. *We're going up? Why?* I realize that we're heading to level 0. The exit. My head bubbles with joy and confusion. I'm going to leave.

I snap out of my delighted daze when Rhig grabs my arm, dragging me out of the elevator. I let out a surprised yelp, quickly moving my feet to catch up. His legs are longer than mine, so he walks faster than I do. Two guards stand in the way of the exit, and Rhig approaches them, showing them his badge.

"I was ordered by Bree Pierces to take this child from the education center."

"We weren't told of any order," one of the guards says.

This seems to stump Rhig because he does not respond. I don't think he thought this far ahead. No offense to Rhig, but he isn't the brightest bulb on the Christmas tree. I could step in, but nothing I say would make a difference. A smirk crawls across my face as my new and improved escape plan comes to mind.

I break free of Rhig's grasp with one twist of the wrist. It doesn't seem like he was really trying to fight it. I turn to the guards and start kicking, punching, and hitting my way to the door. I use all the techniques that Luis taught me, but I've never fought an armed person before, let alone two. My efforts, it seems, have no effect on the Y-DOP suits. All I'm doing is exhausting myself.

Rhig, whom I expect to have my back, stands there, frozen.

The guards hesitate for a moment, then swiftly take out the familiar small, glass box that I now know is a high-frequency taser. I step back quickly. One of the guards, who I recognize as Edwards from the ambush at the theater a month ago, seems to remember me, as well. She whispers something that I cannot hear into an earpiece, and I take the opportunity to grab the taser in her hand. She yells for backup, and I slowly retreat, pointing the taser at anyone who comes near. The guards slowly advance and I grab Rhig's hand, stepping into the elevator. He follows, though I can tell he's scared for his life.

We go to Floor Three. Taking deep breaths, I realize that I'm shaking and have no plan. *Why am I going to Floor Three? I have no idea what's there.* My stupidity will land us somewhere in an office, or worse, a training room for Y-DOP agents. When the door opens, I quickly step off. Rhig says nothing.

We are in a coral-painted hallway, lined with white doors with barred windows. I peek in one, and Rhig does the same two feet above me. It's a lab. The next is a programming room. The next is surveillance. The next is a medical room. The one after that is a weapons room. I smirk.

This was the perfect place to land. The elevator down the hall dings, notifying us that someone is coming. I jump at the sound and

Rhig looks terrified. We duck into the programming room. I can't imagine what he's thinking. He has a child at home. He can't risk any trouble with Y-DOP. My smirk falls, and in the heat of the moment, I say something I might regret.

"You trust me, right, Rhig?"

"What?"

"You heard me. Quick, answer."

He stammers, but then comes up with a simple, "Yes!"

I narrow my eyes gravely. "Listen to me closely. I'm going to need you to break my arm."

He stares at me in shock. "W-what?"

"You took me this far, and thanks for that, but I need you to break my arm. Tell them you were my hostage, and you broke my arm to slow me down. You can go home to your daughter, Frieda, and I may be closer to my escape."

Rhig knows this is no time to argue. He presses his lips together, taking my left arm in both hands. His Y-DOP-issued suit will help him with the job. He looks away, his hands trembling. I pity him. He didn't ask for this. But if I'm going to have any chance of getting out of here, I'll have to make sacrifices.

I can hear the elevator ding again. The agents will be here any moment. *Let's hope this works.* Unluckily, he's struggling. He needs a push.

"Now!" I yell. Rhig closes his eyes tightly.

Snap.

CHAPTER 20

I look around at my new room, in the medical wing of Y-DOP, from the comfort of a plastic, cushioned bed. After Rhig took charge during the attempted escape, I couldn't take the pain and passed out. The next thing I knew, I was being carried to the nurse in a gurney. That was three days ago.

My arm is broken, yes, but this is a huge step forward compared to the past month. For starters, I'm on less of a schedule. There are no cameras in the recovery rooms, though I know they've planted a bug somewhere so they can monitor me. Rhig has hopefully gotten off with a slap on the wrist and forgotten about me by now.

I'm on my own, once again. The best way to be.

An iridescent bird soars by the window. I smile. My mother and I used to go to the pet store by the digital art gallery once a month, to see if the owner had brought any new and exotic birds.

"What if we could let all of these animals out of their cages, and just let them go crazy, even for a day?" my mom said once.

I laughed at her then, but now I feel like those animals in the pet store. Caged.

I've already inspected the window. It's bulletproof, and there's a small alarm on the side of the windowpane that might go off if I try to escape.

But not all is lost. I have a plan that's sure to get me out. I hope. I have one chance, and if I get caught, I'll be stuck on Sublevel 5 for the rest of my life. *Isolated Care* isn't worth my spit. There's nothing *caring* about it. I'd rather slam my head into a door. All I need to do now is channel my emotions into an escape plan. Luckily for me, I know exactly how I'm going to do it.

Annie-style.

Every Sunday afternoon, mom and I would pick a classic movie from her childhood, because she told me, jokingly, that if we didn't, I'd become a "typical misinformed teenager" who "knows nothing about the good old days." I must have watched *Annie* twelve times.

An orphan girl wants to flee her sad life in Ms. Hannigan's orphanage, so she jumps into a laundry cart and rides it all the way to the streets. Annie doesn't make it very far in the movie, but I will.

A laundry cart makes its rounds every two days for clothing and bedsheets. Today, the cart should swing by around noon, which—according to the clock mounted above the door—is in precisely eighteen minutes.

I spend the time flipping through channels on the monitor beside my bed. It swivels in front of my face when I pull it over, making it easier to watch the door out of the corner of my eye. Finally, a familiar burly, crooked-nosed man enters pushing a cloth cart, a sugar-sweet expression painted on his face.

Rhig.

"What are you doing here?" I say, louder than I mean to. This room does not need any more attention than it already has. An attempted escapee and a man bigger than the door he burst through. I paw the monitor out of my face, pushing myself up with my non-injured arm.

"Stop asking questions," he whispers. "Charlie, get in the cart."

I know better than to waste time with small talk. Clutching my casted arm, I hop into the cart. Rhig covers me with bed sheets and pillowcases, which I can only hope are clean. Rhig shuffles around the room for a moment or two while I quickly try to suppress my breathing.

When I've nearly had all I can stand of this muffled shuffling, we start moving. A sharp turn pushes me into the side of the cloth wall, and I have to grip onto the metal frame on the bottom of the cart to keep myself from toppling it over. There is a stop, and my stomach flips as the ground shoots up. Elevators are so much more sickening when you can't see where you're going.

I push some of the pillowcases and sheets out of the way to make a peephole. A group of two or three Y-DOP workers in lab coats are discussing something about pH levels in the pipe system. Rhig is staring straight ahead, his giant arms nervously shaking the cart.

Hey! Look over here! I'm harboring a fugitive!

The scenery changes when the elevator stops, and the doors open. Rhig turns into an anchor-gray, stone hallway with dim yellow lights hanging from the ceiling. Rhig ducks away from the lights to ensure he won't be hit, and I cover my face once again. The hallway is about as loud as an empty graveyard.

Rhig pulls the blankets off me, and I take a much-needed breath of dust-filled air. My throat clutches and I cough out the inhaled dust. Rhig apologizes as he helps me climb out of the cart. He slides open a large compartment on the wall, stuffing the bedding down a metal slide.

"Got demoted to laundry attendant," he says finally. "They didn't have enough evidence to prove I was helping you, but that didn't stop them from keeping me away from the kids. I'll miss taking care of them, but maybe I'll be trusted again by the bosses in a few years."

I give a weak smile. What can I say? I can't help him. I'm focused on my own survival right now.

"So . . ." I start.

Rhig reads my expression. "This is it."

"Yeah."

We say nothing for a moment, then Rhig reaches into his pocket, pulling out a metallic, pea-green watch. He holds it out to show me a crescent-moon-shaped screen glistening sadly in the dim lighting.

"What's this?"

"It's a heat-tracking watch. Quite expensive on the black market, but my cousin was able to get his hands on one."

"What does it do?"

"It's kind of a map. It analyzes the space around you by satellite, twenty feet away at the most, and tells you if there's a living being roaming around." He clicks a dot on the side, and it flickers on, showing a gray outline of the room we're in. Two red blobs stand near the wall of the outline, one slightly bigger than the other. It's me and Rhig.

He continues: "I wanted to give it to you. Y'know, if you're going to be doing all of that running. Might as well know if you're safe."

"Wow, I—" I mean to say I appreciate the gift, but nothing comes out. I haven't had a gift like this in what seems like forever. It's not like I have anyone looking out for me anymore.

"It's how I get away with so much. Bringing back food for the kids, playing board games at midnight when everyone should be in their rooms. The kids deserve fun. Charlie, it's the least I can do for y—"

"No, the least you can do for me is get me out of this dump." I retort, hiding tears with a slight smirk. We share a laugh.

"I'd be happy to." He hands me the watch.

"Now, tell me this escape plan of yours." I clip the watch on, watching the black, unblinking screen.

"Well, the laundry chute."

His confidence makes me look up. Rhig expects me to *what*? Dive through a laundry chute headfirst? What if I'm hurt? What if I'm caught? *What if I'm too late to stop Bree?*

"Rhig, I can't . . ."

"It's your only chance. All laundry goes through a conveyor belt system. Just jump off the belt before you get thrown into a washing machine or the fire and run out the back door."

I blanch. "Fire? What are you talking about?"

"Uh, it's nothing, really. The sheets are scanned right after being dropped down the chute, and if they are too dirty or damaged to be cleaned, they go straight into an incinerator. You probably won't have to worry about it."

My jaw drops. "Nope. I can't do this. I can't."

"Just be careful and you won't have to worry—"

"I can't!" I repeat, louder than before. My hand quickly covers my mouth. I don't want to be the reason I get caught a second time.

"Why not?"

I mumble in reply.

"What was that?"

Incoherent mumbles once again.

"Charlie, I can't hear—"

"I just hate fire, okay?" I yell.

Rhig only watches me with a naive stare. I take a deep breath, lessening the intensity of my headache.

"I—" I take another breath, "—I have since last year. It's a long story, and I'd rather not talk about it."

"Well, okay," his eyes search the room for an answer. "This is your only way out. I'm sorry."

"What?"

His face hardens into cement. "When I was squeamish at the idea of breaking your arm, you gave me a shove. Now you need one, too. Go down the laundry chute or spend the rest of your life here like me. You'd be great at a desk job. Or maybe you could be an electrician."

"That's not fair." My stubborn side takes over, my face mirroring his.

"Life isn't fair, Charlie. But the least we can do is work our way around the pesky little rocks in the road that slow us down. Take the opportunity I'm giving you or go back to Sublevel 1.5."

I take a deep breath, stepping closer to the laundry chute. If I step any closer, I feel that it would suck me in like a vacuum. This did not happen in *Annie*. Rhig gives me a small push—yes, a literal push—and I stumble toward the open compartment in the wall.

"Rhig . . . thank you."

"See you on the outside."

And I disappear into the slide.

CHAPTER 21

Although the fall lasts only a few seconds, it feels like a lifetime. I try my best to suppress my screams, though I can't say it worked. I land, not so softly, on a metal conveyor belt. Holding my throbbing, bandaged arm, I sit up. I am in a large industrial room filled with clothing, bed sheets, and pillowcases moving through machinery on conveyor belts and being hung back up by more machines. I wasn't aware Y-DOP was part *Dystopian Laundromat*.

Remembering Rhig's warning, I look ahead just in time to see the scanner I'm heading toward. A metal box with a red and green light above it. Pieces of cloth are scanned one by one, and a light flashes on, either red or green, and determines where it goes. I quickly look at the bed sheet I'm sitting on.

Oh, good lord.

A giant white cloth covered in yellow, blue, orange, and purple paint. This must be from one of the many arts and crafts activities on the housing floors. There's no way this isn't going in the incinerator. Which means I am, too, if I stay here.

The metal box comes closer, calling to me in not a whisper, but a shout, and I grab the side of it, holding on for dear life. I pull myself onto the ground a few feet below, landing with a *thud* and a weird noise from my mouth.

I look for a way out. The bright red *EXIT* sign glistens above a metal door. Finally, some hope. I check my heat-tracking watch. No one's around. I exit through the door, finding myself in a muddy alleyway. Freedom—actual freedom—for the first time in a month. No creepy scientists in snow-white lab coats, or white walls, or white at *all*. Just natural, unpurified mud.

White is the color of cleanliness, protection, innocence, light, and beginnings. But this is my beginning. Away from the white walls and clothes. Into a world of color and truth. I'm sick of the lies at Y-DOP headquarters. Time to put the past in the past and focus on what's important.

Mom's murder. What a peppy subject.

I start to walk, formulating a plan. Orson, Bree, and Luis expect me to stand by while they figure out the murder, but those idiots won't get anywhere. And Bree is going to try and put off the case so she can exploit the Y-DOP kids, using their memories to grow her program, while simultaneously making them relive all their tragic pasts and traumas.

She's going to try to steal the EASY program unless I can stop her first. I have no idea whether she already has the program, but if she doesn't, I have a window to steal EASY before she can get her slimy claws on it.

The precinct comes into view—the old, disgusting, possibly-haunted precinct. Through my past year serving time, I learned a thing or two about the building. For the first eight months, I was mostly getting caffeine pills for the cops, mopping up after long nights, printing files for detectives, and taking out the trash. Who knew that could come in handy?

I move to the back of the building. My hand brushes against the moldy, vine-covered brick wall, and the traditional back door glistens under its awning. I type the number seven, four times. It's not the password, but it's a trick Honey taught me in my first week, after Orson refused to give me the code. The cracked screen blinks green after a moment. As my hand stretches out to the chipped handle, a breeze kicks up, blowing my hair in my face. *It's now or never.*

As I pull the door open and enter, the scent of old paper and pencil shavings fills my nostrils. Honestly, it's a relief to be in a place I know. After losing my home, the precinct, and even the theater, I needed a win. This is it. Chattering from the close-yet-so-far interrogation room fills the precinct. Music to my ears.

"We'll send Luis back to the crime scene to review footage from the past week. Bree, keep your eyes peeled for any information this guy gives us in his memories," Orson says. My stomach twists at the sound of Bree's name, but I push my fear deep into the depths of my mind, hoping it'll never return.

There is a twinkle of hope. Orson is telling Bree to read someone's memories. That means the EASY program is still in the precinct. I feel like jumping up and down and singing, and I would if doing so wouldn't blow my cover. So . . . I wait.

Their conversation continues, and from my safe corner by the back door, unseen, I can survey everyone's actions. Detectives and interns are working at computers or touch-screen tables, discussing evidence. Luis exits the interrogation room, smiling at Honey Adler as he leaves the precinct. Orson follows, running to the kitchen for a quick lunch. I'll just have to wait for Bree to leave so I can get the EASY program, unless—

Her eyes glance to the corner I'm hiding in, and she smirks. My throat closes up.

She knows I'm here. Of course she does. Her guards have no doubt been watching my every move. Maybe there were cameras I missed in the laundromat. Maybe the trick from *Annie* was too obvious. She could have let me get away. She could have noticed my absence from the medical wing, followed the laundry cart's movements, and rushed to the precinct in a hovercar before I could get here.

This is the perfect opportunity for me to steal the program. The only problem is, it's the perfect opportunity for her to steal it as well. A tiny genius who just had to ruin *my* life. Well, now I have two options. Wait for her to leave, which may never happen, or confront her. The latter sounds far more effective, seeing as Luis, and possibly Orson, will stand by me.

Slowly stepping toward the door to the interrogation room, I take a final breath of ink-smelling air. I enter the room and there she is— Bree, tinkering with the carefully placed wires of the EASY system. I clear my throat, and her head darts up.

"I was just—" Bree's eyes narrow as she realizes who's standing in front of her. She rises, dropping the cords attached to the computer.

"Nice of you to finally join the party. I was worried you'd never get here."

"How did you know?"

"When my guards told me the medical wing was empty, I took a lucky guess. Well? Who broke you out?"

"Let's just say I had a friend or two on the inside."

"That caretaker, Rhig? Why am I not surprised?" she says, sighing as if I'm simply an inconvenience to her plan.

"Bree, you used to be such a sweet person. What happened?" I hope to thaw a chip off her ice-cold heart.

"You are such an idiot." Her response takes me aback. "Once Luis explained his idea for the EASY program to me, I saw an opportunity to expand it and help children around the globe. So I contacted Y-DOP, and they agreed to work with me to bring justice to every child in their center. It got a bit out of my hands, but I'll fix it."

"I just don't understand. Isn't this, the work you're doing in the precinct, enough? Why do you need to hurt these kids?"

She grips the back of the desk chair, locking her eyes onto mine and throwing away the key. "They don't know what's good for them, and neither do you, it seems. What's a little pain created by a memory from the past, compared to a lifetime of satisfaction, knowing the use of your traumas has helped someone else?"

"It's not right."

"Well, it's a good thing this isn't up to you, then." She slowly raises her arm, with a small, white remote in her hand, and I can hear the exit click behind me.

Before I can blink, I am on the floor and Bree is on top of me. I thrash, trying to break free from her grasp, but she is stronger than I expected. Almost too strong. Her sleeve rolls up an inch while I'm fighting, revealing a familiar piece of material underneath her clothes. A Y-DOP suit.

Her strength crushes my arm, and she covers my mouth before I can cry out. My cast can't handle this much pressure. She clasps plastic handcuffs around my wrists. *This situation feels familiar.* Having pinned me down, Bree snatches a vial from the counter. A vial that I recognize. A vial that contains a liquid with a nanochip connected to the EASY program. Bree grabs me by the neck, force-feeding the contents of the vial down my throat. I cough, hearing static.

And Bree slowly fades away.

CHAPTER 22

I decide to skip breakfast and toss a quick "love you" to my mom as I head to school.

Wait. This seems familiar.

Mom?

Mom.

I must be in the EASY program. I try to turn back but am met with a tiny electric shock. That won't stop me, though. I try to turn again, but an even more intense shock shoots through me, and I make my way to school. Tears brim in my eyes. Not in the simulation's eyes, but I can feel it within me. This will be easier if I just stick to the memory and give Bree what she wants.

Jumping the fence, as usual, I land on my feet, kicking up the dust beneath me. The city is more alive now, and bullet trains whoosh past, getting people to where they need to go. One foot in front of the other, I approach the modern-looking, glass exterior of the high school.

My peers walk through the halls, talking and joking around, and I can watch from the outside, looking in. The windows keep every student on display, so no secrets are hidden inside. But it also keeps us at a distance, a clear barrier from the world. I step through the weapons detector in the door, getting the green light to enter.

This is a waste of time. I could have my paws on the program by now and find out who my mom's murderer is. Why is Bree going back to this day, anyway?

Without warning, I freeze in my tracks, and the chatter surrounding me ceases. The students in the hall are motionless, and I have an out-of-body view of the hallway. For a moment I'm confused. I've never seen a third-person view from the EASY program before, but back in training, Bree showed me how to merge memory code with security camera footage. It feels . . . tingly. The space around me shifts, and I can see everyone, including myself, frozen in the moment.

Bree is surveying the hallway at this moment, and I haven't the slightest idea why. She unpauses the scene, and I feel thrown back into my body, my view becoming first-person again. When the voice comes over the loudspeaker, announcing that everyone should get to class, I wait, like I always do, for the hallway to clear.

Bree freezes the memory a second time, and I'm looking through the lens of an omniscient perspective once again. This time, though, there is something I did not notice before. Someone is reaching into my back pocket, taking out the key to my home. A boy. Not just any boy—

Noah.

I start to panic. This isn't a dream. It's real this time. Sure, it's only a memory, but this actually happened. The person I despise most—a foot from me—and I had no idea. The scene around me unpauses and I start to run through the hallways, away from Noah. The walls start to fade to black around me, and the floor falls away. It's just me, running toward nothingness.

I'm ripped from the memory and my entire body aches. After a moment, my eyes open, and I'm shaking. It takes me a full minute to realize my unbroken arm, both feet, and entire torso are secured to the chair in the center of the interrogation room. Stark-white walls and a two-way mirror close me in.

Wonderful, this is just what I needed.

Hot tears run down my cheeks as I try to stop trembling.

A purple-and-black blur rushes in through the door, deformed by the tears in my eyes. The blur wraps its arms around me, pulling me into a hug. A gray blob, shorter than the purple-and-black blur, starts to undo the thick plastic bands holding me down. I wipe my face with my hand to see a worried expression on Luis' face. Orson has his arms crossed beside Luis, watching me nervously.

"What happened? Are you okay?" Luis says, sounding worried.

"You were locked in the memory for over an hour," Orson pitches in, "And we weren't able to get in the room."

"H-huh? An hour? What are you t-talking about?" I say, shivering. It feels as if all of my body's warmth has left me.

"Your memory was playing over and over. Didn't you know?" Orson helps me up. My legs feel like jelly, and I have to put my hand on his arm for support.

I shake my head at Orson's question because that's all I can manage for now.

Luis searches through the computer and his eyes widen. "You remember everything from your memory, don't you?"

"Y-yes, why?"

"We've never replayed a memory more than once. The experience must have stayed in your mind. God—"

"She can hardly walk," Orson interrupts. "The girl needs rest."

In about ten minutes, I am sitting in Honey Adler's swivel chair with a mug of green tea in my hand, Luis, Orson, and Honey, all watching me. Orson is pressing his fists against the desk, Luis stands completely still with his arms crossed, hovering over me, and Honey is crouching beside me, her lip quivering.

"That must have been torture, you poor child," Honey says, brushing the hair out of my face, which was sticking to my cheeks with cold sweat.

"Adler. How about you go do a coffee run?" says Orson, stuffing his hands into his pockets. She nods, fixing her frumpy orange clothes, then quickly waddles out of the precinct.

"Charlie, talk to us," Luis whispers.

"Yes, tell us, Starborne," Orson agrees. "What happened?"

I look up at them, weighing whether to spill the truth or not. There's no telling whether they'd believe Bree, a trusted, government-hired genius, or me, the teenaged, untrustworthy runaway delinquent. I could tell them about Noah, about Bree trying to exploit the Y-DOP children, everything she'd just put me through, and how she's going to do the same to every orphan or victim she can find, or I could be sensible.

But there is another choice. One that wouldn't require telling them anything and would hand me the EASY program on a silver platter. My eyes rise, and I set the tea mug on the desk in front of me.

"I think I might know who killed my mom."

CHAPTER 23

My almond-colored hair flings by my face in wisps, the rain weighing down the heavier locks. I can feel Luis and Orson's eyes burning into the back of my head, and I turn to glare at them. This is the first time I've ever been on a train, and I won't let them spoil it by staring at me the entire trip.

"What?" I hiss.

"Nothing," Luis responds, hugging the briefcase that holds the treasure, the EASY program. "It's just—I don't think either of us have ever seen someone so . . ."

"Excited. Excited to be on a train," Orson finishes for him.

I roll my eyes, staring back out the open window. The shore, a mile in the distance now, sparkles burnt orange, red, and the color of a wine that I barely recognize. Leaves litter the grass, and because of a perfect combination of rain and sunlight, the land on the horizon looks magical. The large body of water between the land and the train reflects the sun in the west, making the water glow amber. Raindrops hitting the surface create ripples that distort the color. I take a mental snapshot for later.

Inspired by the view, my eyes widen. I rise from my seat, stepping out into the wide aisle. Orson quickly grabs my wrist, causing me to look at him.

"Where are you going?" says Orson.

"Wherever I want. Why do you care, anyway?"

"Be careful, and be back before we get to the station."

I hesitate, then, through clenched teeth, respond, "Fine."

My eyes dart around the cabin as I make my way to the restrooms, still on edge. After I explained everything—well, almost everything—to Luis, Orson, and Honey, Luis tracked down Noah through his purchase of train tickets. Like a coward, he was hiding in the city across the river. So, we packed a few changes of clothes and stopped at a store for anything we thought we might need.

I open my bag and look at the contents inside. Without telling Orson or Luis, I had bought scissors, a hair curler, rubber gloves, and a metal container of instant hair dye. My heart beats in my ears and I quickly zip the bag back up again, looking for a restroom stall with a green light on the panel of the door. Finding one closer to the end, I press the panel, the door sliding open. I step inside and walk up to the hexagonal mirror, setting my bag on the counter.

Pressing my palms on the counter, I stare at my reflection, taking one last look at the old Charlotte Starborne. *It's time for a change, and this is one hell of a way to do it.* A smirk creeps across my face, lining my cheekbones, and I stare into my own eyes, my rebellious hair refusing to remain straight. *Goodbye, Charlotte. Hello, Charlie.*

The scissors work their way through my hair, strands falling onto the dark floor. My smile widens as the cutting continues. I have no idea why I didn't do this months ago. Mom would have liked this. Minimalistic, yet complicated. That's one of the reasons I loved her. She was the person I've always wanted to be. I can't forget, however, to leave a piece of myself in the image. I don't cut my hair as short as hers, in a pixie style. Instead, I settle for a simple, beautiful, wavy bob. Brushing my fingers through my hair, I create a side part on the left side of my head. *Perfect.*

Next, the hair dye. I slip a glove onto one hand. It will be hard to color my hair with a broken arm, but I'll manage. Reaching into the bag again, I take the metal hair dye container out, then reach in once more for a capsule I brought with me. I pop the neon orange EarthKey pill into my mouth, waiting for it to dissolve. My playlist starts and I bob my head to the familiar music. I press the panel in the wall, and a chair slides out of it, in front of the full-body mirror.

I sit down and my hand works through strands of my hair in careful movements. The dye dries onto my hair immediately, softening the places it touches. One last touch is needed. I take the hair curler out of my bag, flipping the switch on. The small screen on the side offers choices. Wavy, curly, coiled, etc. I click *Curly* and hold the curler up to my head. I wrap some of my hair around it and the curler starts its work, making my hair as presentable as possible. I only have to wrap locks of hair around the curler, and it does most of the work. After a few minutes, it flashes green, then turns itself off.

Not wasting a moment, I press the panel in the wall again and the chair retracts itself. Another touch on the panel and a large screen opens. I stand still as it scans me. The reflection glosses over, and my age, gender, height, and weight appear on the screen. When my measurements are complete, the rectangle slides the "mirror" aside, revealing a clothing rack, slowly spinning.

I explore the options in the train's mini shopping mall. I choose a simple white shirt, a comfortable, brown trench coat, black pants, and a new pair of laced boots. Zipping the trench coat over my shirt and lacing the boots, I stand to stare at my reborn image in the mirror.

I look brand-new. A curly, brown bob with a side part and light caramel highlights frame my face in a way I've never seen. The trench coat fits me perfectly, as do the pants and shoes. I look not like a former criminal looking for her mother's murderer, but a confident woman with a purpose. Finally, a purpose.

The beeping from the wall jerks me out of my fantasy, and I hold my digital cube up to the panel's scanner. It recognizes Luis' card number, glows green, and accepts my purchase. Luis set it up after discovering I had no money. There is a knock on the door and I quickly stuff everything back into the bag—my old clothes, the hair curler, the dye, the dirty gloves, and the scissors. I zip the bag back up and slide the door open, avoiding eye contact with the person waiting outside. I walk past them, going back to my seat.

Orson is asleep in his chair as I sit down, setting the bag in the seat next to me. Luis looks up from his portable computer. His eyebrows furrow and he glances at the bag beside me.

"Charlotte?" he says after what seemed like a full minute.

"I prefer Charlie."

Luis leans back, taking me in. He elbows Orson, who snorts awake and mumbles curses about his back hurting. Orson looks beside him, and Luis nods to me. Fixing his tie, Orson looks over and blinks. I look back at him with a small smile.

"Starborne, what happened to you?"

"I finally made a change."

"But Charlie," Luis says, putting his computer away, "Don't you feel like you've had enough change in your life already? You shouldn't overwhelm yourself."

"You don't get to decide what's enough for me," I growl back at him. "Neither of you do. I *wanted* this change. This is the first time in over a year that I've been able to choose for myself. I didn't want to get caught for arson, I didn't want to do time at the precinct, I didn't want to work on the EASY program, I didn't want to live at Y-DOP, and I certainly didn't want my mom to die!"

Luis and Orson stare. I take a much-needed breath.

"What happened, happened, and I can't fix that," I say after a moment.

"Starborne, you shouldn't—" Orson starts, but I interrupt him.

"All I can do now is move on, and you two should accept that. For *me.*"

They exchange worried glances, and a voice comes over the loudspeaker, announcing that we've arrived in Carbonstown. I fling my bag over my shoulder, standing, and Luis does the same. Orson stands, takes a giant stretch, and grabs his bag.

We're one step closer to Noah.

CHAPTER 24

"I have to say, Starborne, you've earned my respect!" Orson calls from the bathroom. He had barked at Luis just a few minutes earlier for walking in while he was shaving. "Suffering through the EASY program for that long, taking down a coworker, taking on your mother's case! Have to say, though, could've lived without the makeover."

I rub my hand over my face, tossing my bag onto the floor. The hotel room is small enough to make anyone claustrophobic. Luis takes his shoes off, flopping onto his king-sized bed. I suggested taking the couch, but Orson insisted I take one of the two beds.

"Leave her alone, Bennet!" says Luis, snapping back at his boss.

I can't help but smirk. It was nice to have someone stand up for me, especially to that bossy hyena. Pulling the drapes open, I sit on my bed. It's comfortable, but I'd like nothing better than to be back in my own bed. I fling myself back onto the pillows, taking hold of the closest one to me. Luis sits up, and the pillow meets his face, sending him off the bed. I let a laugh escape my lips, and Luis stands, narrowing his eyes.

"You think you're stronger than me? Let's hope you remember your training, Charlie." A small smile reaches his eyes, and he picks up a pillow, throwing it toward me. I hop up onto my bed, avoiding the hit. Kicking another pillow toward him, a grin spreads to the corners of my face. We continue this war for a few minutes before Orson storms back in wearing a robe, his hair dripping shampoo and water, a towel hanging over his shoulders.

"Would you two knock it off?!"

Luis and I glance at each other, bursting into laughter.

"This isn't the behavior I expect from the best agents in our precinct," Orson huffs.

"You don't look so dignified yourself, Bennet," Luis says through fits of chuckles, eyeing Orson's hair.

"I don't need to explain myself to you—"

"Wait," I stand, taking a pillow out of Luis' hands, "did you just call me an agent? I haven't agreed to that."

"So you're saying you *don't* want the job?" Orson raises an eyebrow.

I look at the ground, clutching the pillow in my hand. Should I go back to the precinct, the place I've despised for so long? I sit on the couch, my eyes glued to the ground. *Should I?*

"I'll think about it."

"No rush. Don't feel pressured—"

"Orson, do you really think telling me not to feel pressured will help?"

My comment shuts him up, and I lie on the couch. I don't need his job offers, nor his bed, nor his pity. I've come so far, I shouldn't stop now. But a sigh escapes me, and I stare at the ceiling. The gross, water-damaged ceiling. I think of one thing. Something I've tried to avoid for months. *The future.* I spend so much energy focusing on my past, while time pushes me toward my future. There's nothing I can do to avoid that.

"Forget the job," I say. Orson and Luis look at me. "What am I supposed to do after this?"

"What do you mean?" Luis asks.

"I have no home, no money, and with Y-DOP after me, you can be sure that I won't get any of that anytime soon. We can't tiptoe around the fact that I'm an orphan. My mom is dead. She has been for a while." The words choke me. "And my dad disowned me over a year ago."

Orson shakes his head, walking back into the bathroom. There are no words now. Luis opens his mouth to say something but stops. There's no point in trying to comfort a person who hasn't finished grieving yet. I desire justice, and I don't care what Noah's excuse is.

After a moment or two, Orson walks back in, shampoo gone, and tells Luis that they need to discuss the case.

"Can I come, too?" I ask, sounding like a child who wants an invite to the cool kid's birthday party.

"This doesn't concern you, Charlie," Orson says.

"Yes, it does!" My brow furrows. I can't help but fight back. "*My* mom, *my* revenge, *my* fight."

They ignore me. Orson nods at the laptop on the bed across from me. Luis goes to get it, but I snatch it into my hands.

"Charlie, you really don't want to see this—"

"Shh!" I hiss.

Orson and Luis both try to take it from me. I break away, run into the bathroom, and command the door to lock. I see Orson and Luis' faces contort, then disappear as the barrier slides between us.

The outside of the sealed laptop blinks on, asking for a passcode. It only takes a minute to enter the security code, Luis' brother's name, *Theodore*. Upon opening, the screen welcomes me as *Luis B. Fysher*. Files slowly appear on the screen, and I click on one labeled *Autopsy Photos*.

I scream before I realize what's happening. The laptop falls out of my hands and onto the cold floor. I can hear Luis' voice from the other side of the door, but I put my hands over my face, leaning against the wall. My back touches the wall screen and the panel blinks green, opening the door once again.

The two bumbling idiots rush in. Luis darts toward me, and Orson darts for the laptop. I sink to the floor, feeling like a black hole has dragged me into the painful abyss of distress all over again. Luis mumbles reassuring words and Orson tips the laptop into Luis' view. I glance up. The screen is glitching green. I broke it when I dropped it to the floor. Luis sighs. I'm sure he'd yell if I didn't seem as broken as his poor laptop.

"I should get to bed," I say, shaking, but manage to get to my feet. "We've got a long day ahead of us."

Not waiting for a response, I walk out, leaving them alone. I don't think I'll be able to sleep naturally tonight, but that's no problem. Using the screen above the bed, I am offered a long list of options. *Drinks, Room Service, Masseuse, Sleeping Medication—*

I click on *Sleeping Medication*, and in a few moments, the screen slides up, presenting a clear container. I take it, empty the contents onto the bed, and send the container back through the wall. I pocket the lozenges and walk to the bathroom for a drink of water.

Luis is gone, probably working to fix the computer in this floor's common room. Orson walks out, glancing at me as he goes past. I stare at the ground, entering the bathroom after him.

The faucet turns on as I pass my hand under it. I pool water in my hands, then splash my face. I shudder at my reflection, my face dripping. I take a sip of refreshing water, then quickly toss the lozenges into my mouth. They dissolve on my tongue. Before I leave the bathroom, I dab my face with a towel, making sure any signs of tears or sweat aren't visible.

I turn to walk into the bedroom but quickly press myself against the wall when I see the scene inside. Orson is sitting on one of the beds, propped up by pillows, almost chugging a bottle of whiskey. I peek into the room once again, tensing up at the thought of my inconsideration.

How bad of a person am I, really? I didn't bat an eye when Luis showed me his living situation. Now Orson is drinking like it's nobody's business, and I can only think of myself. Shaking myself off, I make my way to the couch, not meeting Orson's eyes. I lie down, taking a discreet look at him.

He looks tired. *So* tired. As if he hasn't slept since this whole EASY program chaos started, and I was none the wiser. It's no wonder that he's started drinking. Not to mention that my attitude must be tiring from someone else's perspective. I bury my face in my hands, heating up in shame.

This situation is ever-changing, unprecedented, and never-ending. I spiral every time I think I'm getting somewhere. It's like—it's like I'm taking one step forward and seven steps back. Like I'm in a cave, with the only sunlight filtering in from above, and no matter how hard I try to climb to freedom, I fall back down.

I'm sure it's just the Sleeping Medication talking, thinking up similes. I'll wake up, we'll get Noah, and everything will be perfect. I'll have my justice, get over my grief, and finally rid that monster from my life. That rotten, ugly, stained-heart monster.

I can't wait until all of this is over.

CHAPTER 25

I am woken the next morning by Luis pacing around the hotel room. Papers, file folders, and a duct-taped laptop are scattered across his bed. The purple bags under his eyes suggest he never slept. If Luis hadn't woken me up with his incessant stomping, Orson's hungover snores would have done the trick. I push myself up, putting a hand in between my eyes and the blinding morning light.

This catches Luis' attention. His bloodshot eyes flick toward me like he's been waiting to spout out urgent information for hours.

"Charlie, thank goodness you're awake—" He is interrupted by one of Orson's rattling snores.

"Is something wrong? Did Noah move?" I try to keep my voice steady. We were so close.

"No, that's not the issue. The precinct just sent me a report. They checked one of Ivy Starb—your mom's coworker's messages. He sent threatening emails to your mom in an attempt to get a promotion she was promised. She took the promotion anyway, then two days later, was killed. We think—"

"You think what?" The anger in my chest begins to bubble. "That her coworker murdered her because of a *promotion?* She would have told me if she was being threatened. It was Noah, I know it was!"

"Charlie, I know how much you must be hurting right now—"

"No, you don't know! You can't possibly understand what I'm going through." If my face gets any hotter, I may set the fire alarm off. "Noah killed her, I can feel it in my gut."

"Grief can blind the best of us."

"You want to abandon Noah as a suspect because of a *hunch?*"

"What we had here was a hunch. There's no proof."

"Then we'll find proof! We made it all the way here. Why stop now?!"

"You'll get over this. Once we find Ivy's murderer, you'll be okay. Like you said, you need closure. Justice. It doesn't matter *who* it turns out to be."

My heart rate spikes, and I overturn a lamp on the nightstand. Orson snorts awake, opening his dreary eyes.

"What's going on— agh! Someone close the drapes!" Orson closes his eyes, flinging his feet off the bed.

"Bennet, you saw the report I sent you?" Luis asks, closing the curtains.

"Yeah, yeah, I saw it," Orson says as he stands, flinching when a clap of thunder shakes the outside world. Storm clouds are rolling in from the distance. "We're taking the train back today."

He mumbles to himself about whether to order a caffeine pill or actual coffee as if I'm not in the room. I growl, and I'm sure that if we lived in a cartoon world, steam would be pouring out of my ears. He decides on a caffeine option and begins complaining to himself again. I don't hear much this time, but I'm sure I heard the words "sneaking in," "idiot detectives," and "Blue Office." Orson orders a mug of coffee and a hangover-minimizing capsule from the wall screen, turning back to Luis.

"Go buy train tickets for three—"

"Two," I correct him.

"What are you talking about, Starborne?" Orson says, looking at me for the first time this morning. He takes his order from the wall screen, tosses the pill in his mouth, then downs it with a sip of coffee.

"I'm not going. It's Noah. I know it is." I watch Orson as he desperately tries to massage his headache out of his brain.

"Charlie, don't stress me out right now." He stands, stretching his arms and legs. "Noah was our only lead, but now we have a more practical option. We can't waste time running after this fantasy of yours."

"He's right," Luis says, starting to pack his things into his bag. "You're powered by a prospect, from a memory you retrieved months ago. You can't even be sure he took your house key. Maybe it was something else. Maybe he was *putting* something into your pocket, and it got lost in the wash."

"I know what I saw!" I yell. "And if you two won't help me, I'm going after Noah alone."

"You shouldn't. You're not in the right headspace for any of this. Your mind is probably tricking you—"

I don't hear the last of what Luis says because I've already grabbed my bag and left the room. They're not stupid. They won't stop me. I'd bite one of their hands if they tried. A smirk crawls to my cheeks, and I pull a digital cube out of my bag. Orson's cube. I haven't used that pick-pocketing trick since that first meeting in the conference room. Turning the corner, I take a break, leaning on the ice dispenser.

The digital cube feels light in my hand as I toss it between my palms. It immediately flickers on, responding to my thumb's touch, and asks for a four-digit passcode. Without batting an eye, I type the security address of the precinct into the cube, and it shows me the home screen. I think I have a knack for figuring out passwords. Kind of like a sixth sense. It's easy to analyze someone and figure out what word or set of numbers they would entrust their secrets to.

I shiver as a breeze washes over me, making the hairs on the back of my neck stand. My mind flashes back to the autopsy files and I grind my teeth, trying to forget the sight of my mother's body on a cold metal table. It makes everything so real. Before today, the situation felt like an out-of-body experience, like it had in the EASY program.

I'm not really here, I tell myself.

But that's a lie. I am really here, and my actions have real consequences. I know I'll have to face that soon, but not now. Definitely not now. Not when I'm so close to Noah. He's practically in my reach. Him and his sandy eyes, his dark hair, his—

I slap myself as hard as I can. I'll definitely have a mark after that, but I can't risk any mind-manipulation. This is what he wants me to think. That sociopath. I had a silly crush—that's all it was. This person killed my mom. I know he did, and I'll prove it. Orson and Luis didn't want to do this the easy way, so now we're doing it *my* way.

Focusing back on the digital cube, I start to scroll through the options: tailor shops, food services, work, work, and more work. Orson needs to get out more. I finally land on a file labeled *Suspect Locations*.

I click on it, then scroll once more until I see *Noah: Ivy Starborne Case*. Inhaling, I open the file, finding a map with an active satellite tracker. *Thank God for satellites*, I think to myself, sucking in my breath.

The dot labeled *Noah* is in an apartment building in West Carbonstown. I move to the internet application, looking up Noah's full name in Carbonstown. Nothing. There is no trace of Noah, which can only mean one thing.

He's crime-hopping.

It's a term used for those who want to stay off the government's radar. They jump from place to place, rid themselves of their last and middle names, pay only in cash or have a friend get necessities for them, and use passcodes, instead of fingerprints or faces, for identification. Crime-hopping is punishable by jail time, but it's nearly impossible to find perpetrators.

I smile slightly, as this new information makes things so much clearer. If I can't catch Noah for the murder of my mom, I can at least catch him for crime-hopping, finally attaining justice for my wrongful arrest last year. Throwing the digital cube back into my bag, I stand, leaving the safety of the hotel.

It's time to catch a criminal.

CHAPTER 26

Several long hover-bus stops later, I'm at a large apartment complex. I get out, throwing my bag over my shoulder. This neighborhood is filled with apartment building after apartment building, all made with old, red brick and at least twelve stories high. Following the half-smudged address written in pen on my hand, I make my way to Complex B-1247.

It's a lot like the rest of the buildings in this complex: beaten down with flickering streetlights in front. Storm clouds warn me to take shelter as I approach the locked entrance, staring at the dozens of call buttons to my right. It would be a mistake to click on Noah's room on the twelfth floor. No need to give him a heads-up.

I dig through my bag, looking for anything that could help me get in. Apartments are high security, much like schools, and I'll need to bring my hacking skills into play. That old trick from the precinct won't work here.

The front door buzzes and I look up. The light above the wall screen is flashing green, and, hesitantly, I reach out. The door slides open at my touch, and I take a step back. Someone let me in.

The door stands wide open. No one is around, so I walk in. This seems like no coincidence. I put one foot in front of the other, slowly stepping toward the elevator. I feel like I've got a frog in my throat, and it keeps getting pushed further and further down my esophagus with each step.

The elevator hisses closed behind me and flashes the number *12* on the screen. The top floor. It starts to travel to the twelfth floor, and I lean against the chilling, metal hand bar behind me. The elevator's security protocols will not allow me to go to any other floor. A visitor can only go to the place they are authorized to visit, meaning it had to have been someone on Noah's floor. It doesn't take long to guess who.

Finally, the door hisses open, an automated voice telling me that I have reached my destination. I step out and it closes once again. There's no turning back now.

Unzipping my bag, I take out Orson's digital cube, quickly typing in the passcode. It unlocks, and I open Noah's file for about the forty-ninth time today. My eyes scan the information until I land on his apartment number. Committing it to memory, I start to walk through the hallways of the brown, carpeted floor.

I get to his apartment, 84001, and press the doorbell. The risk is worth it for the payoff. I wait, but nothing happens. Maybe I got the apartment wrong, or maybe someone else let me up, or maybe . . . maybe Noah is planning my murder behind this door.

I say "maybe" too much for my own good. It's the anxiety talking. Taking a deep breath, I reach for the door. Once again, it slides open at my touch. I trade the digital cube in my hand for the scissors in my bag and proceed cautiously into his apartment with my weapon.

It's utterly silent, a desert island. The apartment is tidy and clean, the bed looks like it hasn't been slept in, and the kitchen sink has no water drops around the edges.

There is no sign of an inhabitant here. Making sure, I check the heat-tracking watch on my wrist (thank you Rhig). No one. Not a single person. If Noah was ever here, he's gone by now. Probably in Mexico or Argentina, hiding out. I sigh, walking back to the tiny living room in this tiny apartment and falling onto the couch with a small *thud.*

Checking, double-checking, and triple-checking the precinct's files, I see no reason why Noah wouldn't be here, nor how he would have known we were searching for him. As I'm looking, the holographic TV projects an image in front of me, causing me to drop the digital cube. I stuff it back into my bag, zipping it. I still keep the scissors out, clutching them for protection.

I nearly drop my weapon, however, when Noah's face appears on the TV screen before me. Noah—his smirk, his sandy eyes, his gross expression, and his malevolent mind, all captured in 108-inch, high-definition holography.

"Hello, Lotta. Nice to see you again. How are you?" he says casually, in his honeyed voice.

"I hate—" I start, but almost immediately, Noah's voice interrupts me.

"No, wait, don't try to respond. This is a prerecorded message." Noah chuckles at his own joke. My blood boils.

Noah continues: "Anyway, I bet you're wondering where I am. I know, I know, you want to find me. Trust me, I want you to find me just as much as you do. Well, the most I can do for you right now is give you a hint. Matches can start the biggest flames, and we might be the best match of them all. Go to the place where our flame burned the brightest." He winks and I mentally gag at the tacky line. "Oh, and one more thing."

Noah holds up a digital cube, which displays a video of a room I don't recognize. There are two women, one of whom I can recognize as Iris, Luis' aunt, and the other is a girl with darker skin. Her raven-black hair is tied into a tight ponytail and purple lipstick paints her lips. They are tied to two chairs, back-to-back, obviously struggling. *Really? Hostages?* A growl escapes me, and Noah's recording does not react.

"Just for a little extra motivation," he says. "I suggest you hurry. See you soon, Lotta."

The TV screen blinks off, the hologram disappearing. I am left awestruck. He's not here. The video recording showed that he was in this room, but he is not now. He left me a message. *A hint.* An easy one, too. Not waiting another moment, I shove the scissors into my bag and head back to the elevator.

I click the button repeatedly until I can't feel my thumb anymore, and when it lets me out on the ground floor, I run out of the building. I move fast as a bullet to the train station, not wanting to take another long trip on the bus. There isn't enough time. *Matches can start the biggest flames, and we might be the best match of them all. Go to the place where our flame burned the brightest.* The school.

Exhausted and out of breath, I reach the train station. A machine at the entrance asks for money for the fare and, not wanting to use any more of Luis' money, I dig through my bag, finding the money card I snatched from my mom's room the last time I was there. I buy a ticket and the card notifies me it still has two dollars. I enter the train. I sit in my seat, my eyes sinking closed as the train starts to pick up speed.

A stranger taps my shoulder, and I shift in my seat, opening my eyes. It's pitch-black outside, and the train has stopped moving. I'm out of Carbonstown and back where I belong. I stand, gather my things, and head out of the train station. Memories start coming back to me, and I sprint to my school.

The workday is over so the building should be empty. Any activities, clubs, or after-school tutoring take place in the community center across the street or online. I walk to the door that leads to Mrs. Griffin's science classroom, remembering that I don't have an employee's badge. *This should be easy.* I take out my personal digital cube, holding it up to the badge scanner. The cube turns itself on, offering a fingerprint reader. Employees who lose their work badge can offer their fingerprints as a form of proving their identity. I don't go through that process since it would never work for me.

I click on the top corner, where it says *Advanced Coding,* and the screen changes, throwing a complicated stream of leaf-green numbers and letters across the cube. I smirk, starting to type frantically.

A few minutes later, the scanner beside the door glows green, and I walk in as the door slides open. I start to move through the halls, wondering where Noah could be. *Where our flame burned the brightest.* I have to think of a specific place. Not just the school.

The locker.

I rush to Ethan's locker.

I met Noah in the hallway after Ethan had knocked his school tablet out of his hands, cracking it. I'd helped Noah tell Mr. Ariosto and we'd been friends ever since. That day, Mr. Ariosto had given us some weird, confusing philosophical quote about the importance of having friends. He also threw in a random warning about knowing who your real friends are. Noah and I rolled our eyes as we walked to European History together, laughing.

I wish I hadn't ignored Mr. Ariosto then.

A small light flies past the locker, and I squint, getting a closer look at the reflection on the door. Something behind me moved. Before I can get a chance to turn around, something heavy and solid hits me in the back of the head. I drop to my knees and fall over onto the hard ground. As I drift out of consciousness, I can see between my fluttering eyelids the figure standing over me.

Noah.

CHAPTER 27

A senseless whining fills my ears, making me wince. My head stings, numb from some type of cold compress placed where I was hit. I sit up, opening my eyes, but find that I can see nothing. Darkness. *Am I blind?* I reach up to touch my eyes and find some type of cloth over them. Pulling it off, I squint, stars twinkling in and out of my vision.

It takes a moment for my eyes to adjust. Eyes half open, I look at the room around me. I'm in the corner, so I get a good view of the space. Shelves with boxes and food cans fill the wall to the right of me, and an old staircase leads to a metal door at the top. The walls and floor are made of stone. I think I'm in a basement. A dark basement.

Using the wall behind me for support, I push myself up, stumbling in confused weariness. I walk slowly to the staircase, nearly tripping over myself and clinging to anything I can. Grabbing onto the post at the bottom of the stairs, I raise a shaking foot to the first step.

"I wouldn't suggest that, Lotta. You might hurt yourself," says a voice.

I freeze, then slowly turn to look behind me, but no one is there. At least, I don't think anyone is. It's too dark to tell.

A light turns on, and my eyes flash to Noah who is watching me with one hand on a light switch at the top of the stairs. My eyes tear away from him to two figures tied in the corner, plastic handcuffs circling their wrists—the scene from the video. One has raven-black hair, tied in a tight ponytail. The other is Iris. They are still in the same position as in the video, scared and traumatized. *Noah really wasn't kidding about the hostages.*

Noah grips a gun, walking over to me. I want to hit him, but I can't muster the strength. My arms and legs tremble as I desperately cling to the stair post.

"What is this?" I growl.

"My romantic gesture!" he shouts, motioning around the room with his free hand, the other holding the gun steady. "Do you like it?"

"Noah," I say with a shaking voice, "did you . . . kill m-my mom?"

"Well of course I did! She was in the way of *you*. Of *us*. Your mother didn't believe in us. We could have been something excellent, *brilliant*, a long time ago, but she was our obstacle."

"What . . . the hell . . . did you do?" I am breathless.

"Oh, Charlotte. I love you," he says, almost in a whisper.

"You have no idea what you've done!" I try to hit him, but his hand catches mine halfway.

"Wrong choice, Lotta."

Noah shoves me to the ground, and I grunt as I hit the concrete floor. He points the gun at Iris and the girl. His brow furrows.

"I love you! I always have. And I beat myself up *every single day* for turning you in. You have to believe me. Say you love me back."

"No—"

"Say it or they die!" He puts his finger on the trigger.

"Noah, this is crazy!" It really is. He has murder in his eyes, morphing the sandy color into a beach fire. It swallows him whole.

"I've done everything for you, Lotta. If anything, I did you a favor!" Noah yells, his eyes bulging. "I did it all because *I love you*. We could be happy! You were brainwashed by Ivy Starborne. *Ivy Starborne*," he spits out her name like it's poison, "was in our way. I visited your house, messaged you, put letters in your mailbox. Do you know what Ivy Starborne did? She deleted the messages, burned the letters over her precious stove, and turned me away. Every. Single. Time. Do you know how humiliating it is to be held from your soulmate by her *mother*?"

He takes a deep breath, but his aim does not falter from its target for a moment.

"Lotta, I promise. It was all for you. I know what you're thinking. You miss her. We can't go back, I know, but we can move forward, Lotta, and end up better than before. You—you know, '*To weep is to make less the depth of grief.*' Remember that? Literature class. When we were friends." He's pleading now. "Think of it, Lotta. Really think, it's what you do best. Your mother was one obstacle we will face. Just one. We can get through it. Together."

"You—" I start, my throat catching my next breath. "You don't love me. You're crazy."

"I AM NOT CRAZY!" he screams, and I roll on my side, pushing myself up. With the help of the stair post, I pull myself to stand. "I am not crazy, Charlotte. I care for you. I've watched you all this time.

Monitored you, waiting for the perfect chance to find my way back to you. One day, one fateful day, I realized your mind had been poisoned by *these saboteurs*."

Noah glares at the two hostages, continuing.

"They brainwashed you, *pressured* you—"

"I barely know them!"

"Those people! The ones you are with every day."

"My . . . friends?"

"They are no friends to you. I have been the only true friend to you. Then it hit me. They're in love with you as well! And we can't have that, can we?"

"What?"

"Rhig and Luis, they are my competition. They tricked you. Those *soul-searching* heart-to-hearts with Rhig. That," he laughs, "*pillow fight* with Luis?"

"How could you have possibly known—"

"Oh, naive girl, you should learn to better hide your location. Why would someone leave their curtains open on a secret mission?"

"You are unbelievable," I say.

"No matter, Lotta. They tried to steal you from me by contaminating your brain with dangerous thoughts."

"You're insane. I don't love you. You should be locked up."

"Insane? Insane? I am the most sane person in this room. It's you who can't listen to reason," he hisses.

"Why are they here?" I say, motioning to Iris and the girl, who are trembling.

"Oh, my smart and naive Charlotte. To get what you want, you take what someone loves. Rhig and Luis love their family, so I took them. They can't stand in the way of us anymore. Lotta, I will do this until we have no obstacles in our way, but you have to learn to move on from these useless victims. Victims are all they're meant to be. We're stronger. Why are you still stuck on your mother?"

"I'm in pain," I yell, "caused by you!"

"You've never experienced true pain," Noah snarls. "My heart broke into pieces the day you were taken by Y-DOP. I couldn't see your beautiful face anymore. I have been in pain every moment of my life, Lotta. I could never reach my parents' high expectations, so they abandoned me. At *seven years old*. I was handed to another family, who fought until they tore our household apart. My adopted father could never put a drink down after that. You have never experienced that pain. You have never experienced the pain of being told that you aren't wanted. Or the pain of getting beaten at school every day for just being the most vulnerable kid in class. I *wish* my mom was dead! I was doing you a favor."

Noah stares at me through pleading, tearful eyes.

"I know I am the sanest person in the room because you are ungrateful. Blind! After all of the things I have clawed through to get to you, to get to this moment, why can't you say you love me?"

"Because I don't," I hiss.

That was a mistake. Noah screams, shutting his eyes as tight as he can. It is a soulless scream, one filled with the torment, agony, and despair of a destroyed mind. He steps toward the hostages and the two grimace.

BANG.

I flinch, eyes searching between the three of us to see who was hit, as my ears ring like church bells. Noah gasps for air, holding his stomach, but it wasn't he who was shot. The girl beside Iris sits as if frozen, eyes wider than the sun. Iris stares ahead, her eyes glossed over. Red liquid seeps through her clothing, in the center of her chest.

"I—" Noah starts, taking a few steps away from the murder. "That was an accident! I didn't mean to . . ."

But what's done is done. There's no coming back from death. My muscles fail me, and I take another hard landing on the floor. Noah stares and so do I. I realize something. *That was Luis' aunt.* I take a gulp of air, tears streaming down my face.

I hear a door open and a shuffle of feet down the steps from above. It's someone I recognize. Orson. He holds a small glass box in his hand—a high-frequency taser. I can see his eyes widen at the scene. Noah turns around, seeing Orson. Taking a deep breath, he composes himself once more.

"Orson Bennet. I should have known you'd come to Lotta's rescue."

"Lotta? What—"

"Me," I say, grabbing my casted arm with my hand. Holding my broken arm for support has become a bad habit. *Wait, my arm must be healed by now. Perfect.* I undo the clamps along the edge of the cast, pulling it off. My arm is paler than before and dry. I clutch it once again, my sensitive wrist sending a jolt of pain up my arm. I pull my hand away, looking back to Orson.

Orson reaches for Noah to tase him, but Noah points the gun at him. Orson freezes. I try to drag my feet back up, but I am paralyzed by the situation.

"Walking is a privilege, Bennet!" Noah shouts. Though his hands are violently shaking, he pulls the trigger once more.

BANG.

"Orson!" I scream, but he can't hear me.

Orson is on the floor, clutching his leg. Luckily, Noah's hands were shaking so much he didn't hit Orson fatally. Well, I hope he didn't.

Adrenaline rushing through me, I stand, and Noah looks at me. I start to walk toward him, step by step, trying not to fall over. My entire body crackles with a rage I've never felt before. I am looking at the face of a murderer. *My mother's* murderer. Shouldn't revenge be mine?

I want to release the animal that has been caged inside of me for so long. The animal that bites, scratches, and claws. The animal that wants violence and chaos. The animal that knows what Noah deserves is to be *ripped to pieces.* His heart may be black as coal and dead, but he is alive and more dangerous than ever.

"Charlotte," he says. "I would never hurt you."

"Then put the gun down."

"I can't—"

"Put. The gun. Down. It's over, Noah. You've done enough damage. I could never love you after my mom. After Iris. After Orson. After *this.*"

Slowly, Noah sets the gun in front of him, and I pick it up with both hands to point it at him. I order the murderer to put his hands in the air and kneel on the ground, and he obeys. I'm making this up as I go, but it seems to be working. Being at the precinct for so long has taught me some valuable skills. Maybe I deserve a badge and a black-and-purple uniform. Sweat runs down my face and my voice wavers.

"You're going to the precinct, and they'll deal with you there. We're done, Noah. You scarred me. Left me alone. My mom was all I had. You disgust me, you monster." The gun quivers in my two hands, and I press the emergency button on my watch. Cops should arrive soon.

Our eyes meet and one last tear rolls down my cheek. The tear of letting go.

Right on cue, sirens blare in the distance. But not for me this time. Not for me.

CHAPTER 28

"Frieda? Frieda!" Rhig rushes into the precinct, trying to push through the crowd of officers, detectives, and interns. It's not that difficult for him, though. He's twice the size and twice as strong as everyone in the precinct.

Everyone has rushed from their stations and offices to see what all the fuss is about. Honey Adler is desperately tending to Orson, along with a few medics.

In the chaos, Luis stops one of the officers from the scene.

"I was informed my aunt was a hostage. What happened? Has anyone heard from her? Calliope, please. Anything."

Calliope gives Luis a look of pity and shakes his head. Luis' face drops.

"I—thank you. Excuse me."

Luis covers his mouth with his hand and rushes to the bathroom. I move to follow him, but a few interns and detectives surround me, asking questions and trying to find out exactly what is happening.

I'm finally able to shake them off and turn my focus on Rhig. I grab his hand to lead him to the conference room, where Frieda is hidden safely away from the cacophony of the reception desk. Honey gave her a mug of tea earlier, and Frieda has been in the conference room ever since.

She wasn't very talkative, but I learned her name and connected the dots I had missed back in the basement. This is the daughter Rhig was always talking about. Rhig runs to her, and they pull each other into a warm hug. I smile at them, and Rhig looks over Frieda's shoulder, mouthing "thank you" to me. I leave them alone, pushing back through the crowd to the reception desk. I turn to the group of employees, narrowing my eyes.

"You still have two hours until 8 p.m.!" I announce. "Two more hours of work, so get back to it! The conference and interrogation rooms are off-limits! Go! Chop-chop!" Most leave, going back to their assigned stations, but some roll their eyes. "Orson doesn't pay you to stand around. Move, or you'll have to answer to me!"

Eventually, the rest of the worker bees leave. I press one hand on the reception desk counter to hop over it.

Luis is back, sitting on the desk and staring at the floor with a clenched jaw, while Calliope tries to give him words of comfort about Iris.

"Adler, have you heard anything of Theodore Fysher?" I ask, remembering Luis' little brother.

"Sadly, no," Honey sighs, carefully fixing the bandage around Orson's leg.

"Get me rum or tequila! Or the two mixed together! Now, Adler!" Orson barks, gritting his teeth over the pain.

"I can't do that, Mr. Bennet."

"I'm dyin' over here, Adler!"

"No, sir. The medic said you'd be just fine. You're a lucky duckling, you know. Not all bullets miss the tibia. Would you like to take some Agalferal?" she says sweetly.

"Do I look like I want Agalferal? I was *shot in the leg*! If I had the strength to stand and go to my office, I'd get an Employee Termination Form!"

"Orson, give it a rest. She's trying to help. It's the best she can provide since you refuse hospital treatment," Luis says, his eyes red and puffy and his voice hoarse. "Are you sure you don't want her to take you to the hospital?"

"Dang waste of time," Orson growls. "Now stop saying the word 'hospital' or I'll get a Termination Form for you too, Fysher."

"Fine. I'm going to look for Theodore. I can't take this anymore," Luis says, standing. I would pity him, but the fear of being in a room alone with Noah overpowers any empathy.

"You will not!" I grab his arm. "Help me with Noah. He's waiting, and he may have some information about your brother."

This seems to persuade Luis. He thanks Calliope and follows me to the interrogation room, where Noah sits, restrained, on the other side of the glass. Noah seems to stare straight through it, through *me*, though I know he can't see us. My mind flickers back to Joseph Foster. I shiver, though the room is warm. Luis sits in front of his computer, starting up the EASY program.

"It's still here? Bree didn't take it?" I blink in surprise.

Luis picks up a water bottle and takes a gulp. He clears his throat.

"Of course not. She's smarter than that. The EASY program has its own tracking device. Why would Bree try to steal the program?"

"I—it's a long story, and you wouldn't believe me, anyway."

"Try me." His eyes hold the depths of grief, a look I have seen when looking in the mirror. A wave of trust passes over me.

For the second time, I weigh my options. Who would Luis believe? Bree, a child who is away from the precinct half of the time to God-knows-where, or me, a loyal girl, so desperate to prove herself that she caught a murderer and brought him back to the police. It seems this time, the odds are in my favor. Why not tell Luis? It would feel great to get all this dead weight off my shoulders.

So I tell him. Everything from my plan to steal the EASY program, to getting caught by Y-DOP and spending a month there, to Bree's plan, to Rhig, to the laundry chute, to the incinerator, to my self-inflicted broken arm. He nods as I recap my story, clinging to each word of it.

"Wow, that's—"

"It's all right if you don't believe me."

"Charlie, you're a hero," Luis breathes. That was not the feedback I was expecting. "And I do believe you. It makes sense. Everything makes sense. I just—thank you."

We both look back at Noah in silence. I opened up and the world didn't end. It's astonishing, really. In just over a year, I have gone from criminal to *hero*. He called me a hero. Noah is the one stuck on the other side of the glass this time, and I'm on the side of the law. It's crazy how destinies can be altered in one year.

"Hey," I break the silence, "I'm really sorry about—"

"Please," he interrupts me. "I don't want to talk about it. It's not what I need right now. It's not what Theodore needs."

"I understand more than you know. And I understand that work is an easy distraction. But if you ever need to talk, I'll listen."

"Thank you. No one else in the precinct is making it easy to grieve in peace."

I nod and we stare ahead at Noah in silence again, both waiting for the other to speak.

"Here," Luis speaks up and shoves a vial in my face, "give this to Noah."

"Wait. I have one more question. What happened to the coworker? My mom's? The one that allegedly threatened her."

"Yeah, that was a goose chase. The coworker's account was a complete fake. We were catfished." He chuckles dryly at his own terrible, terrible humor.

A sigh escapes me and I ignore the joke, not wanting to laugh right now. I take the vial, stepping through the door. Noah looks up, and I gaze at one of the bulletproof walls, trying to avoid eye contact.

"Where's Theodore? You must know."

"And if I do? I don't need to tell you anything. What's that law . . . plead the fifth?" Noah smirks.

I raise a fist at him, pretend to swing. "Tell me," I growl.

He flinches. "I don't know who Theodore is."

"You know Luis and Iris. Stop lying!"

"Fine. He wasn't at the theater when I got there. I swear."

"Take this," I say, and offer the vial to Noah. "Drink it."

"I don't want to—"

"Do it!" I yell.

Noah downs the liquid and throws the vial on the ground, where it shatters. I return to the other room, careful to avoid the shards on the floor. Luis is gone. He must have left after getting his answer about Theodore.

I'm alone with the EASY program, and no one is here to stop me from stealing it. After proving mom's murder, I can take off with it. I could break the tracking code, go where I want, helping people just like me. I could help solve Rhig's father's killing. It might not be too late. I could—

I stop myself. I'm starting to sound like Bree. No, I'm the opposite of Bree. I'm not willing to hurt innocents. The only people who deserve this treatment, chained down with their memories being searched, possibly causing trauma and PTSD, are those who have committed the crimes. I can't imagine Bree's world.

I do not want to steal the EASY program anymore. I'm about to have all of the answers to my questions, then I will be free. Sitting in Luis' chair, I can see that he has done everything needed to work the EASY program before leaving. I lean forward, clicking the button to start the memory-analysis process.

"I'm almost there, mom," I whisper.

CHAPTER 29

I already knew what was going to happen. I had seen her autopsy photos and reports. It wasn't asphyxiation or suffocation. I don't care if it took an hour or a minute. I don't care about the cause or the suffering. What matters is that she died. Whatever length of time or amount of pain she was put through, she still died. That's what will make it too much to watch. I don't know if I can bear it.

Still, it needs to be done. *For her.* I scan through Noah's memories around the time of mom's death and nearly trip over my own hands when I see my house. Slamming the Unpause key, then the Recording key, I watch attentively. The familiar movie-like perspective makes it all so real. Seeing my mom, what she said—there's no more guessing, it's all here, a few feet from me. It all started with a knock on the door. Mom's first mistake was answering it.

The door slides open.

"Noah, hello. I'm sorry, but I already told you, you shouldn't come here. Charlotte isn't interested, and frankly, I wouldn't want you around her."

"Please—" Noah's voice oozes through the monitor.

"She's not even here. She's at school, and you should be, too."

"I won't see Lotta there, and you know it," he snaps back. "She's in higher level courses than me. A different floor of the school."

"I can't do anything about that. It was her choice to move to a more accelerated course. You're smart. Why don't you try to move to a higher ranking?"

Mom was always sweet. Never trying to make someone else feel inferior. She also protected me up until the day she died. She's even doing it now, changing the subject on Noah so they aren't talking about me, anymore. I smile slightly, glancing back into the interrogation room. Noah is still unconscious.

"My dad wouldn't sign the papers for me to move on to the next course. Just—let me see Lotta. I won't cause any trouble. I want to speak to her."

Mom throws one last smile at Noah, her face disappearing as she closes the brown door. Noah growls and punches the post of the porch. He groans, doubling over. Checking his hand, I note that splinters and drops of blood line his knuckles where he hit the wood. My stomach turns, and I dig further into the memory.

Blah, blah, blah, Noah taking the key from me. Noah being late for class. Noah getting called out for being tardy yet again. Noah being mocked by the rest of the class. Noah walking to his next course. Noah being tripped by a classmate in the hallway.

My eyes search and search until, finally, Noah is home. I Unpause once again. He is taking off his watch, his portable tablet, and anything electronic, throwing it all onto his bed along with his EarthKey and digital cube. I hear footsteps in the hallway of his house, and he shoves it all into a container under his bed as a tall, stone-faced man walks in.

This must be Noah's father. His adopted one, anyway. I have heard little about him. Only recently, that he's an unloving alcoholic, heartbroken by his divorce. Before that time in the basement, Noah had always described his family as relics. I had never imagined that Noah would have to hide all of his electronics, though. Is he afraid his father will take them away? Sell them? He's not in poverty, so that would make no sense. It's either that or Noah doesn't want to be tracked.

He doesn't want an electronic device on him so he can commit murder without evidence. We're close—*so* close to the murder—and I have to sit through this stupid conversation to record more proof.

"Sir," Noah says, carefully and discreetly fixing his blankets, so his dad won't notice the container still sticking out from under the bed.

"What, are you a clean freak now? Well, fix up the rest of the room then!" The deep voice snarls. I'm pretty sure I can see his mouth foaming from a corner, but that may be from a sip of the beer he has clenched in his hand.

"I'm going to a study group."

"Like hell you are. Just do your homework here. What's a study group going to do for you?"

"It may help me pass the end-of-course exam. I need those grades for higher education."

His father's words slur more with each passing phrase. "You're not getting any 'higher education.' A brain won't build character. It makes you weak. You'll start overthinking things. You need to be quick on your feet."

I almost jump out of my chair when Noah is backhanded in the face, the crack of skin hitting his cheek echoing in my ears. Noah slowly raises a hand to his cheek, and the red mark on the back of his dad's hand reflects on how much it must have hurt Noah.

"Oh, come on. It didn't hurt that much. Don't be a coward."

"I'm going to that study group, I'm going to pass that test, and then I'll get into a higher education program and get away from you. Isn't that what you want?"

"You're going to be a military man, Noah. Maybe that'll put some sense into that walnut-sized brain of yours." He taps the beer can onto the side of Noah's head.

"I don't want to go into the military."

"Why? They're good men. Besides, it's less bills for me," he chuckles, bringing the can to his mouth. He glances into it. "Empty, darn thing."

He tosses it onto the floor carelessly, turning to walk out. I could skip ahead, but I am mesmerized by the horror of this memory, how often this must have happened to Noah, and how I'm making him relive it right now.

"I'm going to be more than you!" Noah yells. "Get a job, and a house, and a wife who loves me."

This makes his dad stop. He walks back over to Noah, grabs him by the hair, and pulls him to the kitchen. He tosses him onto the floor. "You are *nobody*, and that's how you'll stay. As for a wife, you're hopeless. No one will ever love you," his dad spits out. "A wife? You'd be lucky to date a rock! Even that *friend* of yours left you! Chandler—er—Cherry," His dad starts looking through the fridge, I assume for another drink.

"Charlotte," Noah whispers.

"Yeah, yeah, exactly. Your own parents threw you out like Tuesday garbage. Lydia left 'cause of you. We were fine before you broke us up." He glances down at Noah. "Get up! What are you, a dust mite?"

Noah stands, turning around. He grabs a knife from a utensil holder on the counter and turns back to his dad.

"I'm going to that study group."

"What are you gonna do? Kill me? I'd like to see you try," his dad chuckles dryly. "Fine. Go. But if you're not back before 10:30, I'll skin you alive."

"I'll be the one to decide whether I come back!" Noah screams then runs out, still holding the knife.

I chew on my lip, scrolling through the memories for what is hopefully the final time tonight. That knife. The *murder weapon*.

Noah walks to my house in the next memory, holding the key up to the door. A red scanner travels over it, sliding the door open, and he slithers inside. I know I'm not home. That day, I was on Dexter Thomas's case. The day I wasn't there for her.

He sneaks through my home, making his way to my mom's home office, where she is facing the window on the other side of the room, on her work computer. She can't see him. I want to scream at her to look behind her, but it would do no good. Ivy Starborne is toast.

Noah reaches around her neck with the knife positioned in his hand, the teeth facing toward her throat. She freezes, stiffening like a board. I can't help but do the same. *What would anyone do? Why can't she get out? GET OUT. SAVE YOURSELF.* She moves, and he pulls the knife sideways.

I close my eyes, my screams drowning out any sounds from the monitor. Lucky for me, this room is soundproof when the door is closed. It's just me, an unconscious Noah, and a memory of my mom. This is where the memory ends. I keep my eyes shut for another minute or two, opening them when I hear a final, deafening, heart-stopping silence.

My mom lies face-up on the floor in a pool of blood. I see stab wounds on her neck and chest. This is it. My questions have been answered, but I don't feel any better. There are no butterflies, no rainbows, and no marching bands congratulating me for solving the murder against all odds.

It takes a few minutes for my heart rate to slow, and for my hiccups and sobs to stop. I stop the recording and the EASY program saves the memory automatically. I send the file to Honey and turn the computer off.

I wipe my face with my coat and walk to the reception desk. Orson has gone to the Blue Office, or, hopefully, a hospital, and Honey Adler is back in her chair, typing away.

"Adler, when Luis gets back, get him to write a report on the EASY program file," I tell her. "It'll appear in your inbox soon. I urge you to not open it, though I can't stop you from reviewing the footage if you decide to." My voice is raw and dead. "Get an officer or two to take Noah. I don't need anything else from him. And if Orson asks, I'm on a walk to clear my head."

I speak in such an orderly fashion, she cannot comment. I exit the precinct, almost running into Luis, who is holding Theodore's hand. Theodore stares up at me, his rosy cheeks glowing. He looks like he was just crying. My eyes must have the same tired sadness in them. I wave, then meet Luis' eyes in an understanding manner. Finding Theodore was no simple task.

"Where was he?" I ask.

"Hiding in the storage room of Iris's workplace. He was in the rafters when Noah took Iris, then rushed to the grocery store for help. It was her shift, so no one was there, and he just took cover." Luis' face contorts. "The place got robbed. No one was watching over it."

"At least he's safe."

"Yeah. Did you use the EASY program?"

"The file's waiting for you inside."

"Great."

There's a moment of silence. Not good silence, like when you're lying in the grass and there's no one around to bother you. Weird silence, like a demon just happened to be passing by and decided to suck all your conversation skills out of you, before hurrying on his way. So much for small talk.

"We don't have to pretend like everything's all right, you know," Luis says, after what I think is thirty seconds of solid nothingness.

"I know," is all I reply.

He walks inside, Theodore following in his footsteps, and I watch the doors close behind them. I take a deep breath, stepping away from the precinct. I stare at my watch: 8:02 p.m. *How long was I in the interrogation room?* Well, it wouldn't hurt to challenge myself right now. I may need a jog. Or a run. Or a sprint.

Why not race time itself? I set the timer on my watch to ten minutes and get in racing position. I could have been in cross-country if I felt like talking to the sports snobs at school. My watch beeps, signaling me to start. I take off sprinting, my feet pounding on the ground with a relaxing sense of freedom. I don't go on runs anymore. It's sad, but I've managed. It's not like I've had the time or energy, anyway.

Finally, I make it to my house. My old house. My new-old house? Just forget it. I'm here. Home. Except it isn't home anymore, but a not-so-distant memory. I pant, my lungs and chest heaving, and decide to take the fence to the side of my home. I hop it, unafraid of what waits on the other side for once. I know this place. I know it will protect me. I open the back door, stepping inside.

I walk through the kitchen, my room, the bathrooms, closets, and TV room. I stop at the entrance of my mom's office and turn into her bedroom at the last minute. *I'm not ready. I never will be.* My hand reaches for my mom's pillow and my shoes rest on the carpet where she bled. My fingertips graze the pillow when a voice calls out:

"Charlie Starborne."

CHAPTER 30

Is it a ghost? A hallucination? Have I finally gone crazy? A woman's voice calls to me. I whip around to see who caused the noise, only to find that I haven't gone insane. It's Bree, and she's holding a knife. How ironic, considering where I am. Not only a knife, but she's wearing a dove-white, Y-DOP pantsuit.

"You're coming with me," she says. "Back to Y-DOP. You should have never left. I'm going to solve this Noah case—"

"It's solved, Bree. Noah is gone. He's gone."

Her face drops. She growls, turning a pile of dusty books over.

"Months! I have been trying for two months! It's the only murder the precinct had, and I couldn't solve it! *You?* Why you?"

"I barely had to look, really. He came looking for me."

Bree moves closer with the knife, and I step back, holding my palms out in front of me. I imagine her as a predator, and I'm now the prey. Her mission is over, and she needs a new target.

"You know," I start carefully, "you could just forget about Y-DOP.

Go back to the precinct, solve the crimes there, be a hero. You don't need to steal the EASY program."

"Steal the program? You think I still want to steal the program?" Bree laughs. "I'm over that. I'll make my own. That's no problem. The only thing I *can't* deal with is you. So persistent, always getting in my way. And I can't exactly have you running around the streets, an orphan, carrying all of that confidential information about the EASY program around in your head. What if you decided to tell someone? Y-DOP can't take that risk."

"What? But the rest of the orphans? How will they—"

"All Y-DOP children used in the EASY program will stay there indefinitely. Working as employees, officers, etcetera, etcetera, etcetera. Just like your friend, Rhig. He took a vow of silence. We certainly can't have anyone roaming around, spilling information on the things we put the children through. Like you, for example. Do you think I'm going to trust you to not tell everyone you can about Y-DOP's next big step?"

"I have been through the EASY program, Bree. It's horrible. You shouldn't be trying it on children. And you shouldn't condemn them to Y-DOP forever, out of fear that they'll tell someone about their trauma."

"I will make a difference. I am going to be someone worthy of being put on a pedestal. People will write history books about me. Orson and Luis haven't thought about the implications. They don't realize that the EASY program can be used on a wider scale. If only they would put their pride aside and let a few kids suffer for the greater good."

"This is wrong. You can't use people, then lock them up for their own   defense."

"Watch me, Charlie. There will be a change. A shift. And it starts with you."

Bree advances on me with the knife. I push a small garbage bin in her way as a small obstacle. I run out to the street, Bree following close behind. Sprinting as fast as I can, I can hear her footsteps gaining speed. *I forgot she's wearing a Y-DOP suit. She's faster than me.*

Rain pounds on my shoulders like tiny icicles. Spikes that weigh me down and make my feet lose traction but give Bree an advantage. I glance behind me, and Bree's mouth is moving, probably speaking commands into her suit. A van appears in my way and stops directly in the middle of the road. I slam into it, seeing stars in my vision, accompanied by the thumping of the rain.

I stumble back, my head aching, and Bree catches me. Her arms clamp around my stomach, squeezing me tighter than any human should be able to do. She tosses me into the back of the van. The door closes behind me. The vehicle begins to move, throwing me against the rear wall with a metallic thud.

A long drive later, the back door reopens. I jump out, kicking the first person I see. But it's just Bree. She lets out a yelp, and I leave her on the ground. I run. Bree has brought me back to the Y-DOP headquarters. At least I'm familiar with the place.

A lightbulb flickers on in my brain, and I run to a back door I recognize. I swing it open, rushing inside to meet the smell of laundry detergent and clean clothes. I am in the giant, industrial laundry room. A place Bree probably isn't that familiar with. I hop into a pile of not-yet-folded bedsheets, digging a hole among the fabrics as an eye hole to see out.

Bree slinks through the monstrous room, her eyes darting from side to side. She looks in my direction, and I hide my face in the sheets, checking my heat-tracking watch. She is heading in the opposite direction. There are only two red blobs on the small screen. It's just us.

I could stay here, but I doubt it would do me any good. I crawl out of the mountain of bedsheets, prowling after Bree, using the machines and fabric piles as cover.

She turns, sees me, and runs toward me, knife in her hand. I know she doesn't want to kill me, but she certainly looks like she might be planning to. My back heats up like I'm about to fall into the sun. I start to tip back as she stands over me with the knife. I panic, grabbing her arm. Without thinking, I twist her arm and push her, swinging us both around. She screams, and I look behind me. My eyes widen when I see the incinerator. Bree falls in. She actually *falls in*, and it's all my fault. Into the fire, out of existence. I watch, horrified, as flames consume her. I want to cover my ears to silence her shrieking. To shut my eyes to stop seeing her flailing as her skin peels. To close my nose to stop the smell of charred flesh. But I'm frozen, so I watch.

The open door was my mistake. The heater was left open, unattended, and I killed her without realizing it. Bree's voice slowly fades out of existence.

That was me. I did that. I'm a murderer.

No. I'm no murderer. That was self-defense. Yes, self-defense. That was self-defense.

It doesn't seem real. None of this does. I crouch on the floor, cradling my head in my hands, taking heavy breaths, but it's not working. *It's not working.* I can't breathe. It's too much, too much, too much.

This is all too much. Will I be taken into the precinct? Should I even tell them? Bree was a bad person, yes, but she didn't deserve to die. My mom didn't deserve to die. Iris didn't deserve to die.

I don't want to go to jail. I won't go to jail. It was self-defense. She was going to hurt me. Bree was after me. She was going to put me back underground. Back on Sublevel 1.5. I don't want to go back to the housing floor. I don't want to be here, in Y-DOP, all alone. That's what I am now. Alone. And it's my fault. All my fault. I caused this.

I have to get out.

CHAPTER 31

Murderer, murderer, murderer. The word reverberates in my ears, sending chills down my spine. The rain continues to pound against my face, my shoes, and my hands. I could move to the overhang just a few feet away, but I'm cemented to the pavement beneath me. The waiting is unbearable. I'd messaged Honey, without explaining anything that had happened in the past few minutes, and she told me she was sending a vehicle.

"We're coming for you, sweetie. You'll be all right," she had said, as if she understood. *Sure, you understand. You think you do.* Adults pretend they understand to comfort those they deem as naive. I am not one of those kids. It's a front people put up to avoid a greater conflict. To circumvent any issues that could surface. They have their own lives, their own jobs. Why deal with the things some kid has to cry about?

A police siren whines, the sound advancing. *Great. I can't get the sound out of my head.* But it's not just my imagination. A black-and-purple hovercar halts in front of me, splashing water onto my shoes. Officer Calliope rolls the window down.

"I'm sorry, Miss Starborne," she says.

"No need to be sorry. I'd do anything to get out of this rain." I climb into the car, rain dripping from my coat. The plastic strap of the seatbelt buckles over me, and I pull myself together, making sure that there is no sign of tears on my face. Though it'd be hard to tell tears from the rain, at a second glance, my puffy, red eyes and hot cheeks would give me away. The car starts moving, rocking softly. I lean back, rubbing my sore eyes.

We reach the precinct, and I thank Calliope. I walk up to the precinct and a voice stops me.

"Lotta," someone says. It wasn't Calliope.

I look toward the voice. Noah sits in a police car at the curb, plastic handcuffs securing his wrists and legs, two seatbelts crisscrossing his chest, and one more fastened over his waist. The car door is open while a female officer finishes securing the back seat.

"*Noah*," I hiss, straightening my spine instinctively.

"Relax. They're just moving me somewhere. They haven't told me where yet. Some secondary location to keep me until court."

"It won't be a long trial," I scoff. "You've already proven your guilt."

"Charlie, I hope you know that I still love y—"

"Stop."

"I'll never stop. Sure, we've had a little bit of a setback. I might get thirty years. But I plan to wait. I'll always love y—"

I storm over and my fist meets his nose in one great, overhand blow. A sloppy move, I'll admit, but I can't be blamed. It's been one heck of a day. He grunts, and I lean back, resting my head on the carpeted ledge beside the window, my eyes focused on the soft ceiling. It's not like Noah can fight back, and there's no telling whether he'd want the option.

The female officer glances back at us, ignoring the blood running from Noah's nose. It wasn't payback, but it was something. The justice system will take over now. He will be completely out of my hands.

After a moment, the officer warns me about hurting convicts, and I take one *last* look at Noah. He's the same as when I first met him. Broken, weak, but a fighter. I hope he survives in jail. I leave him alone, blood still flowing from his nose, and head to the reception desk.

Honey is on her computer with Rhig standing over her, watching her work. Rhig looks like a kid in a candy store. He starts to pick up glass boxes with slideshows, decorated rocks, toys, and anything else on her desk he can mess with. I bet he hasn't experienced this much in a long time. Honey snatches a Newton's Cradle from Rhig, glaring at him. He stretches over her, reaching for the pens. She smacks his hand, and I approach cautiously.

"Orson and Luis?"

"Blue Office," they both say.

I nod, walking to Orson's famous Blue Office. He rarely lets anyone in there. It's basically his sanctuary. His giant, blueberry-colored haven. The perfect place to ignore every coworker and employee he has. I walk in without knocking or speaking to the man at the desk outside, the door shutting behind me. Orson and Luis stare at Orson's computer screen, not even noticing me. I clear my throat, and their eyes snap up.

"We were just watching—" Luis says.

"My mom's murder," I finish for him. I could see it in their eyes. Their fear. "I have to talk to both of you."

Without meaning to, my eyes start to well up, and my face burns. I sob. Luis opens his mouth to speak, but I start to cry even harder. Tears run down my face, and I hiccup until my entire body aches. In between hiccups and sobs, I spend the next few minutes explaining everything that had just happened, down to the very last detail I can recall. They listen in horror, and I stop the story abruptly when I get to Noah. I don't want to say anymore.

My lip aches as I bite down on it, waiting in fear for what will happen next. *They're going to send me to jail for real this time. I'm done. Finished. My life is over. I'm Charlie Starborne, the murderer with amazing style.*

Orson just presses the call button on his desk communicator and asks his secretary for a towel. I had hardly noticed that I was still soaked from the rain. I had probably tracked it through the entire precinct. A man in a suit walks in with an armful of fluffy towels, sets them on the desk, then leaves.

"Self-defense," Luis says as I wrap a towel around my shoulders.

"I agree. Self-defense. Nothing more," Orson says, smiling tightly. I look between the two men's tense postures. *They're afraid of me. Or in pain from the death of Bree.* "I'll send a report in. No reason to get our hard-working detectives tangled up in this."

"W-what?" My eyes burn in disbelief. "But—I—it was—"

"An accident, and that's how it will stay," Orson says sternly. I don't ask any further questions. "Now, in other news, I'd like to put the offer back out there. Work here, Charlie. You're good at it. Hell, you solved a murder that we couldn't. You stuck with your gut. That's something Luis and I couldn't do."

"I actually wanted to bring that up." I start to chew on my lip again, twirling a corner of the towel between my fingers. "I want to shut down the EASY program. Can you? Please?"

"No," Luis says without hesitation.

"What? Why?"

"Kid," Orson says, leaning back in his chair, "the program helps. Just look at what it's done for us. Foster, Thomas, Noah, and that's just the start."

"I've been on the other side of it. You have no idea what it does."

"So we need to iron out some kinks, sure. It's still new, Starborne. Maybe you've had some bad experiences with the program, but if we can help one, two, a dozen, a hundred, a thousand people, then it's worth it to keep EASY running. We'll continue working on it. It's not perfect."

"And we're not Bree. We know not to go too far. We aren't crossing any lines," Luis says.

"Exactly. And besides, if we do start to cross a line or two, you'll be there to stop us. Right?"

I stare at the wall, their arguments sinking in. They're right. They aren't Bree. They know what too far is. *What would mom want?* She'd want to help everyone she could. Touch one life, and you touch 10,000 more. That's what she told me. Noah negatively impacted so many lives, and I helped by catching him. The EASY program had helped me, and in return, it had helped everyone around me. I can't feel the relief over the pain right now, but maybe, someday, I will.

"Okay," I say softly. "But I'm sorry, Orson. I just can't work here. Y-DOP could still be looking for me. It's too dangerous."

Orson and Luis give me a sad look, and I understand. We've become a team. Friends. We've all been through too much, taken too many hits to split now. I have to do what's best for me, though. I've grown to love the world of the precinct, and the people around me, but I have to stop living in this fantasy. I may feel like I'm missing a part of myself, but after a while, I'll learn to heal. That's something else I've learned here. I can teach my heart to repair itself and replace the cracked parts with steel.

"Is this it, then?" Luis asks.

"I guess so." It hurts to say those words. "I have to stay safe. I can't risk being this close to Y-DOP headquarters. I've already escaped once, and that was only through Rhig's help."

"I heard my name?" Rhig walks in. "I was waiting for an opportunity to come in."

Orson furrows his brow. Rhig might be the largest person he's ever had in his office. So much for a sanctuary.

"Charlie, we should talk," he says. "Y-DOP is letting me go."

"What?" I crane my neck to look up at him. "Why?"

"I shouldn't discuss it, but I know a lot. Seen some things I prob'ly shouldn't have. I finally decided to say something about it. Told them that if they didn't let me go, I'd snitch. They changed their minds after I told them about my connection to the police precinct. They wrote me off after negotiating some terms. Had to sign a contract to keep everything I saw and heard to myself." Rhig scratches the back of his head. "Frieda and I are getting the hell out of Dodge before Y-DOP changes their mind, and if you want to come with us—"

My head snaps to Orson and Luis. Luis smiles, and Orson nods, encouraging me to accept.

"Where are you two going?" I ask.

"I guess we'll figure it out when we get there," Rhig shrugs.

The offer is better than nothing, and it's tempting to think of having a home somewhere. I haven't had a home in a long time. First my house, then the theater, then Y-DOP, then—I guess those are the only three places I've really lived. I could travel. Leave. Finally, like Rhig said, *get the hell out of Dodge.* Someone is handing me the opportunity to break ties to this city. It's everything I could have ever dreamed of.

"When do we leave?"

"Great choice. We leave in one week. I'll buy an extra train ticket." He glances at Orson and Luis over my shoulder. "I'll give you some privacy," Rhig says, smiling, then walks out. The door slides closed behind him.

I look to Orson and Luis. Our goodbyes take less than a minute, summing up our little adventures and tying them up in a neat bow. Luis hugs me, and Orson, not able to stand, just squeezes my hand. They have nothing to give me, nor I, them. So I leave. For good, it seems. I don't know if I'll ever come back, but I certainly won't forget my time here in this old, stupid, crazy, beautiful, caring, powerful precinct.

I make my way to the front desk, where Frieda is wrapped in a blanket, looking like she just woke up from a long nap. Rhig leans against the desk, speaking to Honey. She looks up, runs to me, and pulls me into a smothering hug. I can't breathe through her floral-printed sweater. She brings me away to meet her face, her eyes brimming with tears.

Rhig excuses himself and Frieda, and they leave to wait in the hovercar Rhig ordered. It takes what seems like an hour for Honey to finally let me go. Everyone else has already left.

I've left an imprint on so many lives in my time here. Those are the ones who will remember in the days, weeks, and years after I'm gone.

I retrieve my bag from the interrogation room, looking around one last time. I want to cry, but I won't. There's too much crying that's been done already. No point wasting tears on a room. My hand runs over the computer that holds the EASY program as I walk out—out of the interrogation room, away from the reception desk, and out of the precinct. I can feel the eyes of Orson, Luis, and Honey burning into my back as I leave, but I don't look back. I don't want to look back. If I do, I may decide to stay.

Getting into the hovercar with Rhig and Frieda, I set my bag in my lap, my shoulders relaxing. The precinct gets smaller and smaller, and I may break my neck if I crane it any further to look back. I'll miss it, but who wouldn't?

Goodbye.

CHAPTER 32

"You okay, Charlie?" Rhig asks.

"Yeah. I'm okay," I answer simply.

I shift in my seat, looking out of the window of the train. The sun shines in my eyes, and I close the drapes, looking back to Frieda and Rhig. So much has happened in the past week. On Saturday night, Rhig invited me to stay with his family. Just him, his daughter, his cat, Chubby—the name fits—and me. Rhig told me they were staying here until they found the right moment.

On Sunday, the precinct forwarded me a copy of my mom's will, which I had no idea she had written. Some things went to coworkers and friends, and the house went back to my dad, as he had originally bought it. My mom, who had always wanted comfort and financial stability for me, had set up a special bank account in my name.

Over the years, she had saved $25,000 into the secret account. *Twenty-five thousand.* We had never had that much money in my life. My mom had saved at least a thousand dollars every year since I was born, and it had compounded. I'm sure she wished for more money than that, but her death cut short the payments. Still, it was more than enough. All the money had been automatically transferred into my personal account.

On Monday, Rhig, Frieda, and I spent the day shopping for me, buying new clothes, a new bed, toiletries, and more. After the giant City Mall, we went shopping online and ordered Indian food, that we ate on the couch.

On Tuesday, I introduced *Annie* (along with the two sequels, the one prequel, and the four remakes) to Rhig, Chubby, and Frieda. We had a movie marathon and analyzed each film after they were done.

Wednesday was a day of further relaxation. Frieda introduced me to the sport of Gutterglobe. The game consists of four small trenches in four corners of a field, sixteen players, and eight remote-controlled balls. The game is, to me, weird, but entertaining. Four teams play against one another, and every game lasts fifteen minutes. Each team has two people in a trench playing offense, one controlling two balls with a digital cube, and one runner. The one remote controller tries to get the balls into opposing teams' trenches. The runner kicks opposing teams' balls into their own trenches, causing them to get stuck, and the kickers in the trenches try to kick them out of their own trenches. Blah, blah, blah *sports*. I played with her team and found that I actually have a knack for Gutterglobe. Still, I doubt I'll ever play on an actual team. Maybe if the sport had a cooler name.

Thursday and Friday were all packing—furniture, clothing, everything. I looked around the house with a long sigh. It was yet another home to say goodbye to. I quickly shook the thought away. I'll patch up my heart and find somewhere else. A new home with Rhig, Frieda, and the most loyal family member, Chubby.

Saturday came and it was time to board the train. Rhig helped the attendant throw everything into the baggage hold while Frieda and I mapped out our journey. The train ride would last only a day, but we'd travel all the way to Poppymill Beach, where Frieda says her mother was born.

I watch the calm waves roll past us as the train moves quickly down the wide river. My eyes close, and Rhig and Frieda start to discuss possible housing options. No need to consult me. They could take me anywhere and I'd be happy as a shark when a school of fish swims by.

There's no question about it. *I'm ready.* I am willing to move on and start a new life with promise. Enroll in a new school, find a new home, and connect with my new makeshift family. I don't need to live in the past anymore. Forget the precinct, forget Carbonstown, and forget Y-DOP. The only things I need are the people in front of me, and the cat in the traveling cage in the seat beside me. Minimalistic, just like my idol, my mom. *Yeah, I don't need the precinct. I don't need—*

My watch vibrates, sending a weird buzzing feeling through my wrist. I check it and see a new message. Mail, in a file that's too large to display on the watch. I take my digital cube out of the bag under my feet, opening the message. It's from Luis.

> *Charlie,*
>
> *Orson and I wanted to offer you the job once more. There's a file below, containing a brand-new case. A killing at Y-DOP caused by a fight between a group of children and a few security guards. One of the kids claimed to not be an orphan. Their guardian, the uncle,*

*had left the child unattended outside of a grocery store,
and Y-DOP picked them up, claiming they looked
similar to one of the children they were searching for.
After a day in Y-DOP, the child was refused a phone call
to their guardian and started a fight with the guards. It
ended badly. You would be a strong force on this case.
Get back to us ASAP. -Luis;)*

I open the file, review it quickly, then return to double-check the message. *They don't need me. They want me.* It feels nice to be wanted. I look back to Frieda and Rhig, standing.

"I'm sorry. I have to go."

"What do you mean?" Rhig asks.

"I mean," I take a deep breath, "I'm going back to the precinct. I was a fool for thinking I could just leave."

"Do you really have to?" Frieda asks, disappointment stretching from her eyes to her hands.

I nod. "This was nice, but I've made a home there. I can't just leave."

"Charlie," Rhig says, "come visit us in Poppymill Beach."

"I will." I smile.

"But wait. You can't leave now. We're moving!" Frieda stares at me.

"Don't worry about me. I always find a way." I wink, zipping the waterproof seal over my bag.

Rhig chuckles, and I send a quick message to Luis.

I'll do it.

I think of Noah, and, for some reason, silently thank him. I have built myself back up from rock bottom and have become so much stronger. I opened myself up enough to call people my friends. I learned. I learned how to care, how to survive, and how to laugh. I became a person I'm proud of for once. I am Charlie Starborne, and he, Noah, is the person who made me what I am. I don't love him, but I can't hate him, either.

I run down the aisle, passing unsuspecting passengers and trying to not trip over bags. There's only one way off this train, and it certainly isn't going to stop moving for me. One thing I've learned is that life continues to move as quickly as it can. That doesn't bother me anymore, though. A jump certainly helps to catch up with the next big thing before it catches up to you.

At the back of the train, I pry open a manual metal door on the side of the compartment. The water from the river spurts in at me, droplets splattering the carpet. The body of water passes under me as the train speeds by.

I look both ways to make sure the coast is clear, and the compartment is completely empty. A smirk slithers from my teeth to my cheeks to my nose, and it turns into a delighted grin. A sunbeam warms my ankles, and I fill my lungs with fresh air, pulling my bag closer over my shoulder. My hair flings in every direction from the wind that rushes into the cabin.

I step closer to the edge of the train, wondering what it will feel like when I hit the river below. That's all pain is. You hurt, then you survive.

I've never had trouble with jumping fences. Just a climb and a jump. It's so easy. All you have to do is take a leap of faith. Maybe sometimes there will be an obstacle or a few thorns on the other side, but that's never stopped me, and it shouldn't stop anyone else.

It doesn't matter whether it's a murderer, a fence, a crazy organization, an insane genius, or a dead mom in your way. If you can teach yourself to heal, to forgive, to learn from bad experiences, to face the rain, the obstacles, and the bad days when you feel as if you're sinking, you're unstoppable. Invincible. Indestructible. Allow yourself to be torn down. Allow yourself to feel.

Just look in the mirror, make yourself into the person you've always wanted to be, and paint a brave face on. Show the world what you can be, as if it's one big stage where you can change the story at will. Jump those fences, but don't forget how to open your heart to those who deserve to listen to you. You have to have trust in yourself. Trust in your decisions. Just . . . jump.

And I do. I jump.

FIN

Thank you so much for reading *Starborne*. If you've enjoyed the book, we would be grateful if you would post a review on the bookseller's website. Just a few words is all it takes!

Acknowledgements

Before I begin the thank yous, I would like to shine a spotlight on my best writing partner, who sat beside me for every word, every page, and every email of *Starborne*—my dog, Buddy.

By its very nature, writing is a solo project. But getting any work published requires a world of collaboration. I am fortunate to have so many people who have supported and helped me on this journey.

This novel could not have been possible without the help of many people. My parents, brother, sister, and family have been supportive every step of the way. Thank you to those who helped me become who I am: Robert Katz, Susan Katz, and Robin Katz (Birdie).

Thank you to all of those who, when I began writing books in high school, believed in me: Ashten Ormandy, Kristine Duncan, Dan Crawford, Ann Winstead, Brandon Collins, and Arissa Chennault. Thank you to Melody Daniels for listening to me talk at her desk for years about my publishing dreams, and for being there for me when it finally happened. Thank you to my first Beta reader, Samantha, and to Alyssa Levin, Shaina Maitino, and all others who read *Starborne* as a simple word document. Thank you to all of those who believed in my writing from the start, and stood by me throughout: Jesse David Roberts, Jack Paransky, Miriana Mason, Ben Spiegel, Adrienne Magill, and Ruthie Mitchell. Each one of you has helped this book become what it is now.

Thank you Diana Zorek and Fabiola Caraballo Quijada for taking the craziness and fast-paced world of this story into your own hands.

And a special thank you to those who have helped me into the professional chapter of my writing career. Thank you to an amazing editor and friend, Scott Bury; to William Johnson for his photography; and to all of my mentors in the writing world: the Creative Arts Academy, Creative Writing Coalition, the Yiddish Book Center, and my friends and colleagues at The Writer's Factory (Alex Zielinski, Seth Land, Deanna/Rose, and Fox).

Lastly, I would like to thank the entire team at TouchPoint Press for your time and support, and for giving me the opportunity to tell this story.

I give all the gratitude I can to the readers, advice-givers, mentors, and friends who have made it this far with me. Thank you.

CPSIA information can be obtained
at www.ICGtesting.com
Printed in the USA
BVHW082117300323
661447BV00015B/1026